Massacre

Bolan ran faster after Harding into the main terminal. Suddenly the building exploded into chaos. Bolan heard the chatter of automatic weapons. The gunfire was drowned almost immediately in a sea of screams. All around him, people were falling to the floor. A huge plate-glass window collapsed in shards to Bolan's right. The sharp crack of M-16s had blown out the window.

Bolan hit the deck, his Beretta in hand. He spotted one terrorist in combat fatigues struggling to ram a new clip into an AK-47. Bolan fired once, catching him in the shoulder, and again as he pitched forward.

Feet pounded behind him, and Bolan glanced back to see a handful of airport police charging toward him. An AK opened up and the policemen fell to the hard marble floor all around.

Suddenly it was very quiet. Then, one by one, the wounded began to moan. Panting, Bolan got to his feet. Sirens howled in the distance. Outside, a squeal of brakes announced the belated arrival of reinforcements.

Slowly Bolan walked back to his small suitcase. As he bent to pick it up, two policemen rushed toward him. They were shouting, but Bolan ignored them. Something else had captured his attention.

Fifty feet away, Harding vanished through a doorway. Bolan started to run after him. He didn't feel the first hand to grab his arms. Or the second.

MACK BOLAN.

The Executioner

DON PENDLETON'S
THE **EXECUTIONER**®
FEATURING MACK BOLAN®

WHIPSAW

A GOLD EAGLE BOOK FROM
WORLDWIDE®

TORONTO · NEW YORK · LONDON · PARIS
AMSTERDAM · STOCKHOLM · HAMBURG
ATHENS · MILAN · TOKYO · SYDNEY

First edition December 1990

ISBN 0-373-61144-7

Special thanks and acknowledgment to
Charlie McDade for his contribution to this work.

Printed in U.S.A.

Peace is produced by war.

—Latin proverb

I am involved in an Everlasting War.
But I cherish hopes for ultimate peace.

—Mack Bolan, the Executioner

THE
MACK BOLAN®
LEGEND

Nothing less than a war could have fashioned the destiny of the man called Mack Bolan. Bolan earned the Executioner title in the jungle hell of Vietnam.

But this soldier also wore another name—Sergeant Mercy. He was so tagged because of the compassion he showed to wounded comrades-in-arms and Vietnamese civilians.

Mack Bolan's second tour of duty ended prematurely when he was given emergency leave to return home and bury his family, victims of the Mob. Then he declared a one-man war against the Mafia.

He confronted the Families head-on from coast to coast, and soon a hope of victory began to appear. But Bolan had broken society's every rule. That same society started gunning for this elusive warrior—to no avail.

So Bolan was offered amnesty to work within the system against terrorism. This time, as an employee of Uncle Sam, Bolan became Colonel John Phoenix. With a command center at Stony Man Farm in Virginia, he and his new allies—Able Team and Phoenix Force—waged relentless war on a new adversary: the KGB.

But when his one true love, April Rose, died at the hands of the Soviet terror machine, Bolan severed all ties with Establishment authority.

Now, after a lengthy lone-wolf struggle and much soul-searching, the Executioner has agreed to enter an "arm's-length" alliance with his government once more, reserving the right to pursue personal missions in his Everlasting War.

1

The stink of dead fish swelled up in the alley. His stomach started to churn as he moved into the darkness. He thought for a minute he was going to vomit, and swallowed hard, the bitter taste of the bile rising all the way into his throat until he could taste his last meal along with it.

It was hotter than hell, and the sweat rolled down the back of his neck and trickled under the rounded edge of his shirt neck. He stopped to get control of himself, leaning against the sticky wall.

He took a step away from the wall, and something squeaked. It darted past him, a long, thin tail dragging along the wet pavement. He didn't have to look to know it was a rat. And he didn't have to count to know that there was more than one. They moved in packs, a dozen for each one visible. And it was that, more than anything else, that made him hate the Third World. The damn rats. Why in hell couldn't people take care of their garbage? It wasn't necessary to leave food rotting in alleys for days at a time, until every kind of vermin had a chance to eat its fill. These people were no better than savages.

He took another step, and his foot landed on something soft and squishy. He steeled himself for the familiar smell of dog excrement, but this time he was wrong. Whatever he'd stepped in didn't smell that bad. It was wet and sticky. His shoe made a sucking noise when he lifted it, then some-

thing cloyingly sweet swelled up around him, much like
overripe banana.

As he drew deeper into the alley, the darkness seemed to
suck the heat right out of his blood. He started to feel cold
all over, and he shivered despite the sweat rolling down his
chest and soaking through the underarms of his shirt. He
heard a distant throbbing, like some sort of giant dynamo.
He stopped again to listen, but he couldn't get a fix on it.
The sound rose and fell as if it were stopping and starting,
or as if the wind, or the distant ocean, somehow interfered.

He shrugged it off and took another step, and this time
the dynamo started to get louder. He accidentally kicked a
splintered packing crate, and it fell into a pile of folded
cardboard. The humming suddenly swelled in volume and
broke into a thousand splinters. Then he realized it wasn't
distant at all. It was the flies, sitting like some single,
throbbing thing in a layer on the piled garbage. Their
separate buzzes slashed at him as the insects soared up over
his head, then settled back down.

The noise gradually fell away until once again it sounded
a hundred miles away. The smell of rotting fish grew worse,
as if fanned by a thousand sets of tiny wings. He hated fish,
hated the stink of it, the feel of it on his tongue. He couldn't
think of fish without gagging. And he couldn't take another step in that damn alley without thinking of fish.

He turned his head away, but it was too late. It swelled up
in him like the first rush of oil as the drill breaks through
and taps a new field. He doubled over, and the first wave of
nausea racked him until his stomach hurt. He thought he
would turn inside out. Again and again his intestines tied
themselves in knots, trying to get out. He doubled over and
braced himself with one hand on his knee.

The spasm passed, and he turned to one side to spit out
the horrible, rancid taste. He wished to hell he had a bottle
of beer, a glass of water, anything to rinse it away. And he
knew that he couldn't afford to think about it unless he

wanted another bout of the heaves to sap whatever willpower he had left.

Spitting that awful, dry spit, he shook his head and swallowed hard one more time, sliding past the puddle on the ground. He forgot about the flies now, and even the stink of fish was forgotten. All he wanted to do was to get away from the incontrovertible proof of his own weakness. Giving the mound of garbage a wide berth, he bumped against the wall of the building on his right. It jarred his shoulder, and his teeth clacked together. He thought for a second he'd chipped one, then realized it had been that way for years.

He looked up at the sky, which seemed to have disappeared for a second. Then, like a narrow strip little more than a foot wide, he saw a band of black sprinkled with stars. He realized the eaves of the two buildings arched out over the alley, almost touching in places. It was almost as if he were in a tunnel with a skylight. He felt the walls pressing in on him, and his head started to spin. He closed his eyes to fight off the vertigo, shook his head to clear it and tried once more to concentrate on the business at hand.

Ten feet, he kept telling himself, eight feet, six feet. Step by step, like a scared kid inching past a graveyard, he marked his progress.

In the darkness, in the back of his mind, he kept hearing the squeak of the rats. He shivered, imagining the rodents trying to slither under his cuffs and up his legs. God, how he hated being there. He wondered whether that was why he did what he did, whether he hated such places so much he had a compulsion to obliterate them all, wipe them away as surely and completely as the teacher's pet washing the day's assignments from a blackboard. He asked himself that sort of question often. He never had the answer, but knew it didn't make any difference. He was what he was, and nothing could change him. And it suited him to think of himself that way—immutable, irresistible. He was a force of nature, a fact of life.

He was at the hard part. He could look a man in the eye in broad daylight, and put a bullet right between his eyes. He knew he could because he'd done it. He could design a bomb to look like anything from a Bible to a hair dryer. He'd done that, too. But in the damp dark he felt vulnerable.

He shut his ears to the droning of the flies and groped along the wall until he found the back corner. It was tricky work in the dark, but he couldn't risk using a light. He didn't want to call attention to himself and, more than that, dreaded what unwanted things would be picked out by the beam. At the back corner, he leaned against the wall, taking long, slow breaths through his nose.

In his chest he could feel his heart pounding like an angry fist. The noise of it thumped in his ears, his pulse roaring like white water through a narrow chasm. His mouth felt dry and pasty. It still tasted of bile and the afternoon whiskey. He placed one hand flat against his chest, pressing on his heart, stroking the tight skin under his shirt to calm himself.

When his composure started to return, he ran through it all in his head one last time, just to make sure. He had the right building—he was certain of that. And he had all the equipment he would need. One by one, he ticked off the inventory. He could even visualize the yellow sheet he'd used to assemble it. So meticulous he was that he always wrote everything down. Just to make absolutely certain. Then, item by item, he had gathered the tools of his trade and put them in the nondescript green canvas backpack. Then he'd burned the list.

He imagined every unforeseen contingency and carried tools to deal with them, as well. He was perfect, and he knew it. So did those who employed him. It was why they paid him so well. It was why he could work as little or as much as he chose. But he was superstitious. He never worked during the month of June. It was the month of his birth, as well as his mother's. It was also the month of her death. In his calendar, June was a sacred month, his own personal Ramadan—it was a fixed Lent, a time to reflect on the eleven months that had gone before. He wondered why he had agreed this time to work in June.

In his head he said a little prayer, one of thanks for his success so far, and a petition for safety during the night ahead of him. When the prayer was finished, his heart had returned to normal. He could still feel it, but it was a good feeling, a peaceful, regular rhythm. He was back in control. The rats and the flies were behind him. And there was consolation in the fact that some of them would disappear by the following noon.

He moved quickly, his goal so close that it drew him on like a magnet. His tempo quickened but his heart stayed calm. He was in his element now, the perfect professional. He heard nothing but the noise of his tools on the lock, saw nothing but the outline of his fingers against the dull metal. The lock clicked in almost no time at all, and he tucked the picklock into his back pocket.

The door swung open and bumped into something against the wall. Glass rattled in the ancient wooden frame. He closed it softly, leaving it just ajar so he could pull it open with a snap of his wrist.

Feeling ahead in the darkness, he made his way through the tangled junk in the back room. Old furniture, cartons of paper, several paint cans arranged in a precarious stack. A tall box full of fluorescent bulbs. He almost screamed when his face broke through a spider web, and the broken strands tangled in his hair and tickled his neck and ears. He brushed angrily at them, smacking at the skin of his neck and cheeks.

He found the doorway to the middle room. Here, he knew, there were no windows. He clicked on a small flashlight and set his bag on the floor. Dropping to a squat, he undid the flap and took out the rest of his tools. He worked quickly. This part was the easiest. He liked to tell himself that he could do it with his eyes closed. One of these days, just to see if he was right, he would do it. There was practically no risk, not if you knew what you were doing.

And he did. Better than anybody else.

When he was ready, he put all the tools back and hefted the package in one hand. It felt just about right. Not too heavy for the size of the box, but not so light that it would seem odd. Leaving the flashlight on the floor, he walked to the door leading to the front. He'd come to the hard part—the crucial part.

To get the maximum effect, you had to be precise, even scientific. How to hide something in plain sight was the tricky part. You wanted your handiwork to stay right where you put it. Not only did it have to look as if it belonged, but it also had to look as though it had been right where it was forever. People had to see it without realizing it; they had to take it for granted.

The front room was the largest. There was a little light spilling in from the street, just enough for him to move around without tripping over anything. A long coffee table covered with American magazines sat up front, under the broad plate-glass window. At either end, a low sofa, just big enough for two, or maybe for a mother and two children, filled the remaining free space along the front wall.

He got on his knees and looked under the table. He could probably put it there, but that was too easy. Besides, the table looked heavy and it might interfere. The desk was out, because it would be in the way there.

What about right on the table, he wondered. Maybe with a magazine on top of it, not to conceal it, but just to give it a touch of belonging.

Why not? He asked himself the same question three times. When he could come up with no good reason, he went for it. A copy of *National Geographic* was just the right touch. Sitting at an angle, it showed one corner of the brown paper. But that was perfect. You could worry this sort of thing to death if you let yourself. But he wasn't going to let himself.

He slipped into the back room, picked up his flashlight and grabbed his bag. He was moving smoothly, the uncertainty gone. Out the back door, which he pulled shut. Once more he had to make it past the rats and flies. Knowing they were there made it more repulsive.

He swallowed hard as he tucked the small flashlight back into his pocket. Moving quickly, almost sprinting, he slipped along the alley. He sidestepped the puddle of vomit and nearly slipped and fell.

Once he made the street, he allowed himself to breathe for the first time since reentering the alley. His heart was pounding again, but this time he relished it. Already he could imagine the result of his handiwork. Tomorrow around noon, he would wander by, just to make sure, and peek in to see if he could spy the corner of brown paper.

Then, across the street, his back against the wall of the newsstand, he could reach into his pants. He could already feel the smooth metal, warm from the sunlight on his pocket. He visualized the sudden rainbow of glass, pieces sparkling like fiery jewels as they arced high into the air, caught the sunlight and tumbled back to earth.

It would be good, and it would be the first of many.

2

Walt Wilson was a big man. His two hundred and thirty pounds looked out of place in the Brooks Brothers suit. His bull neck strained against a thirty-dollar silk tie, and his shirt, white on white, rustled every time he shifted his massive torso in the chair.

Mack Bolan watched him quietly. He had met Wilson before. The nickname "Rosebud" seemed out of place on a man so huge, but Bolan had never bothered to ask Wilson where it came from. He preferred instead to let the man have one secret. And for that matter, to Wilson he was Mike Belasko, a friend of Brognola. So he had his own secret, and a high ace it was.

Nor did he envy Wilson his job. A troubleshooter for the Intelligence division of the State Department, Wilson had no place to call home and no base to call his own. Wherever it got hot, Wilson got sent. He seemed to thrive on the challenge, but Bolan knew just how old it could get, and how quickly it could age you. Wilson was on the edge of a downhill slide. The next crisis, or the one after that, could be the one that pushed him over the edge.

The two men sat across from one another with an ocean of gleaming walnut, smelling faintly of lemon oil, between them. At one end of the briefing room, a stark white screen descended with a pneumatic hum. It clicked home, and Wilson nodded to his assistant, who killed the lights.

"First picture," Wilson said in a voice that seemed too high in pitch for someone so large. Bolan wondered whether Wilson's tie might be a little too tight for his own good.

The projector's magazine advance hummed, a bright square of light splashed on the screen, was swept away by a click, reappeared, vanished with another click and was replaced by a photograph of three men. Bolan knew instantly that it had been taken from a distance.

Without waiting for Wilson's question, Bolan scrutinized the three. He knew none by name, although one, the leftmost on the screen, looked vaguely familiar.

"Know any of these rascals?" Wilson asked.

Even in the near dark, Bolan knew that Wilson was watching him closely. "Nope. One guy, the one with the gray hair, looks sort of familiar, as if I should know him. But I can't connect the face with a name."

"Next shot, Donny," Wilson piped.

The projector whirred and clicked, and the photo was replaced by a blowup of one of the three men.

Again, Wilson waited. *"El numero uno."* Wilson chuckled. "That is Juan Rizal Cordero. Ring a bell?"

"No," Bolan said.

"Well, he's the new kid on the block. We've been watching him for more than two years. He shows up at the damnedest places. Nicaragua, two years ago, was the first time we tumbled to him. Right after the attempt on the Ortega brothers. We lost him after that for nearly six months, then he pops up, of all places, in Beirut. Mossad backfilled our file. Seems he's been training the right-wing Christian militia there, sabotage and demo work, mostly. Then he comes out of the ground again last February, a regular fucking ground hog, he is, in Angola. Palling around with a bunch of Woolworth mercs, soldiers of misfortune I call 'em. That was right before Savimbi's plane lost a wing after the ANC conference in Nairobi."

"You tie him to any organization?" Bolan leaned closer to the screen, waiting for Wilson's answer.

"Nope. The boy seems to be a free-lancer. He goes where the bucks are, I guess, but we don't know where he goes to ground. It's now you see him, now you don't. Kind of like a right-wing Carlos, I guess you'd say. Hell, for all I know, maybe he *is* Carlos. Change his nose, add sixty pounds, turn his politics inside out and you got a dead ringer." Wilson laughed in his high, lilting voice while Bolan chewed on his lower lip.

The machine clicked again, and another of the trio appeared center screen. The blowup fuzzed a lot of detail. The man was sitting at an angle to the camera, and his profile was as wispy as breath on a cold afternoon. One prominent, dark eye looked like a burn hole in the screen, but the rest of him was hazy and indistinct.

"Sorry about the quality," Wilson said. "Sometimes I think Fotomat does a better job than our lab."

"Got a name for this one?" Bolan asked.

"Not a syllable." Wilson sighed. "He's new in our rogues' gallery. We don't even know what nationality he is."

Next to fill the screen was the image of the distinguished gray-haired gentleman. He was the one Bolan had seen somewhere but couldn't place or come up with a name.

"If you knew anybody up there, it'd be this fella," Wilson said. "Charles James Anthony Harding."

"Harding," Bolan muttered. "Harding—I know that name."

"Three Purple Hearts, a Bronze Star, a DSC. Four years in a POW camp, courtesy of Uncle Ho. Worked out of a think tank outside of L.A. for a while. Still there as a consultant, but mostly he stays in the Philipines. Did a stint on the Hill, then ran for a House seat in Mississippi, his stomping grounds, but lost by a hair's breadth, and *voilà*, a thinker was born."

"Where were these photos taken?" Bolan asked.

"Manila. Two months ago."

"What's his connection with Cordero?"

"Search me..." Wilson stood up and walked to a sideboard to pour himself a coffee. "You want one?"

"No, thanks," Bolan said, continuing to study the screen.

Wilson scooped two spoons of sugar into the coffee, added a little cream from a silver creamer, then stirred. He set the spoon down with a clang and sipped noisily before returning to the table.

Dropping back into his chair, Wilson set the coffee on the polished tabletop, leaned back to stretch and said through gritted teeth, "Next one, Donny."

Harding disappeared and was replaced by a shattered storefront. Paper-and-cardboard signs, torn to ribbons, fluttered in a breeze at the instant the photo was taken. "This," said Wilson, "used to be a government health clinic, set up by Aquino. Next..." The projector clicked. The storefront moved to a corner of the screen. "See that white circle, down there on the left? Watch this..."

The projector clicked again, and the circle expanded to touch the four sides of the screen. "See that?"

Bolan leaned a little closer.

"It's fuzzier than most, because we got this from a Manila newspaper."

"Cordero," Bolan said.

"Right you are, boyo. Not a minute after the explosion. You can still see smoke in the other corner, just beside the storefront."

"You don't think it was a coincidence, I gather," Bolan said.

"Hell, Belasko, would you?"

"No, I wouldn't."

"And the interesting thing is that this picture was taken just forty-eight hours after that little confab we saw at the beginning. But that's not all... show him, Donny."

Whirring and clunking, the projector advanced another notch. Another photo, this one from the opposite side of the shattered headquarters, filled the screen. "This one is about thirty seconds later. Blowup, Donny..." Wilson skipped a beat, then resumed. "And here you have another of the confabulating buddies, right in the middle of it all, just like Cordero."

And sure enough, in a profile shot, there was the second man, this time just a little more clearly etched.

Bolan said nothing.

Wilson chuckled. "The odds are gettin' pretty long against coincidence, ain't they?"

Wilson took another noisy sip of coffee. "But the pictures ain't the whole story, Belasko. There's a big iceberg under that little bitty ice cube you saw on the screen. It seems that Mr. Harding has been showing up in Manila regularly, twice a month for the last four months, like clockwork. The rest of the time we don't know where the hell he is. It also seems that he has been doing a lot of shipping to the Philippines. It's supposed to be electronic parts, according to the manifests, but I have my doubts about that."

"Why?"

"Well, for one thing, the C-4 that blew that clinic all to hell has been traced to a missing batch from right here in the U.S. of A. Now, I don't know that Harding was behind the theft, but I don't know that he wasn't, either. It makes me a little nervous, though, thinking that he might be. And I am the very picture of calm alongside the Secretary of State. I mean, you can understand that, I guess. After all, how would it look if we were somehow connected to terrorist attacks? And worse yet, in the Philippines? Subic and Clark are not your run-of-the-mill bases. Mrs. Aquino might be a nice lady, but if she thought we were trying to blow her to bits, she might be a little irritated. You ever think how the Pacific would look if it was to be MiG-27s flying into Clark, instead of F-16s? I know the President has, and what he had to say about it is not for polite company."

"So you want me to find out what Harding is up to?"

"Now, hold on, there's more."

Bolan shook his head. "I think I will have a coffee."

"Good move. It's going to be a long night."

Bolan stood and moved around the end of the huge table, fixed himself a coffee and sipped it slowly, leaning against the sideboard. "I'm still missing something here," he said. "I thought the problem in the Philippines was the NPA, the New People's Army..."

"And you were right. It *is* a problem. But it's been manageable so far. The trouble is, if it even looks like we've been supporting the right wing over there, shit will come flying in from every shade of red in the Pacific basin. China and Vietnam, Russia and North Korea, hell, they'll be falling all over themselves to make points with the locals and get themselves a foothold. If that happens, Aquino goes down the tubes in jig time. She's only hanging on by the skin of her teeth. If she goes, there are a dozen generals just waiting for a chance to emulate Mr. Marcos. And if that happens, all hell breaks loose. At best you can have a civil war, and at worst, a red Manila."

"And we take the rap."

Wilson slurped some more coffee down. "Yup." He set the coffee down again, the cup almost sliding off the saucer. "Lights, Donny," he said.

The lights came on, and Wilson reached for a stack of folders, each stamped LA for Limited Access and bordered in bright blue. He spread the fingers of one hand over the top folder. Bolan walked back around the table to sit down.

"This is everything we've got on Cordero. On Harding we don't have much. His life's an open book, sort of. But the pages are blank. You can always see where he's going, and his career's been well documented, but that's all icing. We got no cake underneath. If he's fronting for somebody, we don't know who. If he's got some hidden agenda, we don't have a clue what it is. In other words, if he isn't what he appears to be, what the hell is he?''

Bolan looked at the folders, then at Wilson, who continued. ''Time was, Belasko, when we only had to worry about one end of the political spectrum. Red was easy to spot, like a fire engine coming up the block. If it wasn't red, we didn't have to worry about it. But times have changed in a major way. We've taken a lot of hits, more than we should have if you ask me—but nobody has—and so I now have twice the work to do. I have to watch everything left *and* right.''

Bolan reached out for the folders, and Wilson shoved the stack across the table. ''I wish to God there was more I could give you, but that's what I've got. Period.''

''When do you want me to leave?'' Bolan asked, not bothering to ask the earlier, more obvious question.

Wilson dug inside his jacket and pulled out a crisp white envelope. He slipped it across the table.

Bolan looked at it without making a move to retrieve it. ''Pretty sure of yourself, aren't you?''

Wilson watched the big guy silently for a minute before continuing, ''Brognola speaks very highly of you. He and I go way back. He told me there were certain things I could take for granted. I took him at his word.''

Bolan smiled the faintest of smiles.

''As it happens, you'll be on the same flight as one Mr. Charles Harding. This time we don't want to lose him. You'll be going under diplomatic cover. The man to see in Manila is Frank Henson. I cabled him this afternoon. He knows you're coming, and he'll take care of contact on his end.'' Wilson leaned across the table, extending one hand. Bolan took it in his own. ''You be damn careful over there, Belasko. Anything happens to you, Hal will have my balls in a vise. If he doesn't cut 'em off altogether.''

''Thanks. I'll be careful.''

"Look, Frank Henson's a good man. He's yours for the duration. He knows it and he's as faithful as the family dog. Use him. He expects it, and he'll bust his gut for you."

WHEN THE DOOR CLOSED, Wilson dropped into his chair with a sigh. "Poor son of a bitch," he mumbled.

"You say something?" Donny was busy putting his equipment back in the cabinet.

"Yeah, I said what a poor son of a bitch Belasko was."

"Don't worry about it."

"Sometimes I don't like the things I have to do in this job."

"Yes, you do, Rosebud. You love it. If you didn't, you wouldn't be half as good at your job as you are."

"But we're supposed to be on the same side."

"Walt," Donny said, snapping the cabinet door closed. "If cannon fodder didn't exist, you'd have to invent it. Belasko's cannon fodder, plain and simple. He works out, fine. He doesn't, hey, next case...it's just that simple." He shrugged and closed the door softly behind him.

Wilson sat for a long time, staring at the door. Finally he turned off the light and left the office. All in a day's work, he told himself. And he believed it.

3

Bolan spotted the man immediately. He was taller than average, and his slicked hair shone dully under the overhead light. The last few passengers took their seats after fumbling with carryons and shifted in the uncomfortable closeness of the plane. A slender blonde closed the door, then stepped back to let a male flight attendant seal the hatch tightly.

Bolan watched his quarry out of one eye. The one good thing to be said for a plane was that he didn't have to worry about being shaken off. The blonde went through the mandatory routine, pointing out the various doors, dangling an oxygen mask from one ruby-nailed hand and delivering her spiel with a kind of bored precision just a notch above that of a computer.

When she was finished, she disappeared almost instantly. It was like a magic show. All that was missing was the smoke. Bolan felt warm, and wished the plane's air conditioning would kick in. He had to keep his jacket on to cover the Desert Eagle in its shoulder holster. His diplomatic credentials allowed him to bypass the X-ray rigmarole, but he was almost sorry. He felt small beads of sweat trickle down the back of his neck, then collect at his collar. The sudden surge of air from the overhead vents was even warmer, and he reached up to close his off for a few minutes to give the compressor time to cool the air down.

Bolan buckled his seatbelt as the sign came on and the
arning bell chimed softly somewhere behind him. The en-
nes of the 747 began to whine, the low rumble turning to
snarl, the pitch rising steadily. The cabin floor began to
emble as the big jet backed away from the terminal. Bo-
n glanced out the window at the drooping wings. As often
s he'd flown, it still amazed him that something so huge
nd so heavy could move at all, let alone take to the air. The
lane was lumbering now, its landing gear thumping over
e oozing asphalt expansion joints in the apron.

The engines strained even harder as the plane lurched into
e runway approach, then began to barrel straight ahead.
olan watched the play of the flaps, the polished steel rods
leaming against a background of grease and dull metal.
hen they were up, and the ground started to shrivel away.
he pilot banked sharply, and the runways shrank to a pat-
rn of crossed concrete lines. Los Angeles itself sprawled in
very direction, as if some giant press had flattened a nor-
al city and allowed the ruins to ooze out in every direc-
on.

The cars on the freeways seemed to dissolve in the misty
nog, their exhaust systems cooperating with the climate
nd adding to the mysterious disappearance. With the plane
ver Beverly Hills and Bel Air, the odd-shaped swimming
ools winked up at him, nearly the only things visible on the
round now, their pale blue faces arrayed like some tur-
uoise cryptogram.

Bolan turned away from the view to watch the back of
harles Harding's head. The stylish razor cut looked as if
had just been finished, every strand of hair in place.
Harding was almost a cypher to Bolan, but it was his job to
llow Harding. For three days, ever since Wilson had put
im on the spoor, Bolan had been doing just that.

Whatever it was Harding was supposed to be guilty of, he
ad acted like a man without a care in the world. As Bolan
atched, the older man tilted back in his seat, obviously

planning to spend at least part of the long flight napping
The sound system chimed again, and the seatbelt light wen
out. The No Smoking light followed suit, and a flurry o
flint wheels and matches behind him warned Bolan the ai
would shortly turn blue.

What Bolan knew about Charles Harding he could stuf
into a gnat's ear and have room left over. Wilson hadn'
known, or at least hadn't admitted knowing, very mucl
more. The files were not much more informative. A retired
Air Force colonel, Harding had been a staffer to one of th
more hawkish members of the current Senate. That had
been a short-lived relationship, and Harding had droppec
out of sight for nearly two years, then popped up again a
the executive vice-president of an arms brokerage house, one
with a pipeline to the military and the Congress. After two
years in that position, Harding had resigned to become
executive director of the Federalist Institute, a right-wing
think tank based in Los Angeles. That relationship, too
went by the boards. He was now listed as a consultant by the
Institute. Other than that, there was nothing.

According to Wilson, Harding had lately been doing more
than thinking, and more than a few people on Capitol Hil
wanted to know what. Bolan had resisted the assignmen
initially. It sounded too much like baby-sitting, and Bolar
had neither the inclination nor the patience for that sort o:
work. He didn't like it, wasn't particularly good at it and
usually begged off. But Wilson had done everything shor
of kowtowing to change his mind. Since Brognola had pu
Wilson on to him, and since he owed Brognola one or two
he agreed.

So Bolan sat there, ten rows behind Charles Harding.

And wondered why.

They were still three hours away from Manila wher
Harding stirred in his seat, popped the springs and let the
seat bounce upright. He got to his feet and adjusted his shirt
and tie before stepping into the aisle and moving back ir

Bolan's direction. Everything about Harding, from the rigidity of his spine to the precision of his steps, echoed his years in the Air Force. The service had a way of shaping clay, then baking it so hard that nothing could change it. Even under extreme stress, it would shatter before it would give way.

Harding moved past him, his eyes on the rear rest room, and gave Bolan just the slightest of passing glances. If he had an inkling Bolan was on his tail, he gave no hint. Bolan fished a folded copy of the *Los Angeles Times* out of the seat pocket and opened it to the sports page. Without interest he scanned a story about Tommy Lasorda and the Dodgers, mired in a six-game losing streak, while keeping an ear out for the rest-room latch. When it clicked, Bolan involuntarily stiffened a little. On assignment, he never liked having someone behind him, but on a half-empty jetliner, there was very little he could do about it. Any little thing could give him away.

Harding made his way forward, stopping beside Bolan's seat for a second when the plane hit a spot of turbulence. When the Boeing settled down again, Harding knelt in the aisle to retie a shoelace. He glanced at Bolan for a moment as if trying to make eye contact or to find an opening for conversation, but the big guy kept his eyes glued to the paper.

Harding straightened, then moved on, tucking his shirttail snugly in place under a gleaming leather belt. Bolan watched him take his seat again, half expecting the man to turn and wave, but Harding simply sank into the seat and settled earphones in place to listen to the canned music piped through the plane from a multideck tape player somewhere behind the galley.

The attendants started working their way down the aisles, pushing stainless-steel carts and taking orders for drinks and cardboard food. Harding took a light meal, a Scotch on the rocks and a ginger ale. Bolan settled for some imitation pot roast and wilted vegetables with a carbonated drink.

By the time the attendants had finished cleaning up, the pilot came on the cabin PA system to announce the weather at Manila and to inform the passengers that they were about to begin their descent from thirty one thousand feet. Bolan stood with his back to Harding, took his carryon from the overhead rack and dropped it into the empty seat beside him. After moving to the rear of the cabin, Bolan took a paper cone full of water from the galley, then turned to watch the passengers as he sipped it.

The Fasten Seat Belts sign came on, and the stewardess warned Bolan to return to his seat. Walking down the narrow aisle, he realized that Harding had changed places and was seated much nearer to the front of the plane. Bolan cursed under his breath. He didn't want to risk calling attention to himself by following suit, but Harding had ended up being so close to the front exit that he had a real jump.

Like Bolan himself, Harding had checked no luggage. If he got out of the plane and through the terminal quickly, Bolan might lose him altogether. And he didn't want to think about how difficult it would be to find a single gray-haired needle in the haystack of Manila. Bolan dropped into his seat and cradled his carryon in his lap.

The big Boeing's tires screeched as they made contact, and the plane seemed to collapse in on itself as it lurched along the runway. Bolan unbuckled his seat belt while the light was still on, but didn't stand. If one of the attendants called attention to him, Harding was almost certain to turn around.

The plane taxied toward the terminal, its engines surging as the pilot maneuvered into the accordion dock. Bolan was on his feet a split second before the warning light went out for the final time. Harding was already moving toward the door as the flight crew worked the complicated wheel-and-dog arrangement that kept it closed. Three or four people stepped into the aisle to reach up for their hand luggage, temporarily blocking Bolan's path. He cursed inwardly as the door swung back and Harding disappeared.

Bolan wriggled through the human obstacle course as quickly as he could, provoking more than one irate shove, but he ignored the comments on his rudeness. At the door he stepped into the collapsible rubber tube, his feet ringing hollowly on the metal floor. Harding was already out the other end. Bolan began to run. The tunnel rose and fell under his weight, and he could hear the creaking of its metal joints. It took a sharp left, and began a sharper descent. Bolan plunged into the last leg just as Harding pushed into the main terminal. For a moment he could see the tall man's gray hair bobbing above a sea of people waiting to greet the passengers.

Bolan ran still faster. One arm out like a charging fullback, he plowed through the milling crowd. Harding had reached the outer fringe of the mob now, and his path was relatively unobstructed. Bolan juked to the left to avoid a woman pushing a stroller. For a second he lost sight of Harding again.

Suddenly the terminal exploded into chaos. Bolan heard the chatter of automatic weapons. The gunfire was drowned almost immediately in a sea of screams. All around him, people were falling to the floor, covering their heads with folded arms. Bolan turned to his right to see where the gunmen were. A huge plate-glass window collapsed in shards. The sharp crack of autofire somewhere behind him had blown out the window. Colored paper and a landslide of toys gushed out through the broken glass.

Bolan hit the deck, his Desert Eagle in hand. He spotted one man in combat fatigues, the mottled brown and olive so out of place in the bustling terminal. He drew a bead as the man struggled to ram a new clip into an AK-47. Bolan fired once, catching him in the shoulder, and again as he pitched

forward. A second Kalashnikov opened up from behind a
marble pillar to the dead man's left.

The pounding of feet came from somewhere behind, and
Bolan glanced back to see a handful of airport police
charging toward him. The AK opened up again, and the
policemen fell to the hard marble floor like bowling pins in
the wake of a solid hit.

The cop to his left lay still, a trickle of blood oozing from
his slack jaw. Bolan grabbed the M-16 half-hidden by the
man's prostrate body and tugged it free. Scrambling to his
feet, Bolan charged the pillar, daring the hidden gunman to
step clear. He could see the gunman's crouching back reflected in another plate-glass pane beyond the pillar.

Angling to the left, he cut in a broad circle until enough
of his target was showing. Dropping to one knee, Bolan
brought the M-16 up just as the shooter spotted him. Bolan
tugged the fire control onto full-auto and cut loose. Chunks
of marble flew off the pillar, and the ricochets ripped out the
glass behind it. The gunman pitched forward, and Bolan
swung his muzzle downward, slashing at the extended form
with a short burst. The body twitched for a moment, then
lay still.

It was suddenly very quiet, except for a couple of shards
of glass that tinkled to the floor one by one, but that was all.
The screaming had stopped as if at a director's command.
It seemed almost like it had been that quiet forever. Then the
wounded began to moan, as if they now felt safe to do so.
Panting, Bolan got to his feet, the M-16 dangling from one
hand. He let it drop, and it hit the marble with a dull thud.

Several of the wounded policemen were sitting up. Others,
unharmed themselves, tended to their comrades. Sirens
howled in the distance. Outside, a squeal of brakes announced the belated arrival of reinforcements. There was no
chance of finding Harding now, Bolan thought. Slowly he
walked back to his small suitcase, standing on end where he
had dropped it. As he bent to pick it up, two policemen

rushed toward him. They were shouting, but Bolan ignored them. Something else had captured his attention, something a lot more important.

Fifty feet away he saw Charles Harding, as neat as ever, vanish through a doorway. Bolan dropped his suitcase and started to run. He didn't feel the first hand to grab his arms.

Or the second.

4

Bolan sat in the chair quietly. So far he hadn't been asked to say anything. Roman Collazo, who was, as he stopped frequently to point out, a captain of the Military Police, had been content to do all the talking. Once, during an exceptionally long pause, Bolan leaned forward, but Collazo stopped him with a raised hand. "Not yet, Mr.—" he glanced at the papers in front of him for a second "—Belasko. I'll tell you when."

Bolan leaned back in the chair without a word. If Collazo wanted to challenge Castro for the hot-air record, that was all right with him.

"So, you see," Collazo continued, raising his voice for emphasis, "it is important that you tell us everything you know. I realize that you are here as a representative of your government, and that accordingly you are protected by diplomatic immunity. But I don't think I need to remind you that privilege brings obligation, as well. In this case, the obligation to be as forthcoming as you can. It is essential that we learn what happened, if for no other reason than to ensure that such a thing cannot happen again in Manila."

Collazo paused to look at Bolan over his half lenses. "Am I making myself clear?"

At Bolan's wordless nod, the captain continued. "Good. So, now, Mr. Belasko, if you will," he said, sinking into the tall leather chair behind his desk, "tell me everything you can about what happened at the airport."

"I came out of the debarking tunnel. I was working my way through the crowd when all hell broke loose."

"You mean the shooting?"

"Yeah, the shooting." He looked at Collazo to make certain the man had actually asked such an inane question. There was nothing on the older man's face to suggest he hadn't.

Bolan continued. "At first I couldn't tell where the shooting was coming from. People were falling to the ground, and there was a lot of screaming. It all happened so fast that I wasn't sure whether the people on the floor were seeking cover or had been hit."

"I gather, though, from your prompt reaction, that you are not unfamiliar with gunfire."

"No, I'm not unfamiliar with it." Bolan closed his jaw with a nearly audible snap.

"I see." Collazo leaned back in the chair. "Go on, please..."

"I threw myself on the floor and drew my weapon."

"You are authorized to carry it in your work?"

Bolan nodded. Before Collazo could question him about his work, he pushed on. "I spotted one of the gunmen off to my right. I knew it was a terrorist, not a policeman..."

"Because of the fatigues..."

"Yeah, that, and because he was firing into the crowd. I heard return fire from behind me. I turned and saw it was the police, but I didn't pause to weigh the situation—I just relied on my instincts. So I fired—"

"You didn't think the police were capable of doing their job?"

"It wasn't like that. I reacted and fired. In the back of my mind was the thought that if I didn't, he might get away or he might kill more innocent people. It's a big terminal. The police were still some distance away at that point."

"I don't want you to feel that you have done anything wrong, Mr. Belasko. But—" Collazo spread his hands, palms down, and patted the desktop "—I'm sure you understand."

Bolan gestured vaguely with his hands. Cops were cops, and he wasn't surprised. Hell, he thought, it would be the same hot air and bullshit in Chicago or New York. Why should Manila be any different?

Then Collazo smiled. Bolan didn't like the look. It seemed out of place. And then the captain threw a curveball. "You were traveling alone, Mr. Belasko?"

"Yes." Something told him to be careful, and he tensed. "I was traveling alone."

"I understand that you were running through the terminal even before the shooting started."

"Yeah, I was."

"Do you mind telling me why?"

"Yes, I do."

"Ah," Collazo said, leaning back in the chair and rocking. "I see...." He studied Bolan for a long moment.

Then, as if it had just occurred to him, he asked, "Even though you were traveling alone, did you know anyone else on the plane?"

"Not as far as I know. I didn't see everyone."

"Of course. But of those you did see, was anyone familiar to you?"

Bolan shook his head. What the hell was Collazo after, he wondered. "Look," he said, "if you tell me what you're after, maybe I can help, but this merry-go-round is getting us nowhere."

Collazo was about to respond when the phone on his desk buzzed with the sound of a small, angry wasp. He picked it up impatiently, swiveling the chair until his back was to Bolan. Then, without having said a word, he swiveled back and replaced the phone in its cradle.

"Where are you staying, Mr. Belasko?"

"At the MacArthur. Why?"

Collazo didn't answer him. Instead he remarked, "That's all for today. I'd appreciate it if you'd stop by in a couple of days."

Bolan shook his head. "Whatever you say, Captain."

The big man got to his feet and bent to retrieve his small bag. He studied Collazo for a moment, but the captain was already immersed in paperwork on his desk. If he felt Bolan's eyes on him, he didn't show it.

Bolan opened the door and let it close gently behind him as he stepped into the busy outer office. He'd give his eyeteeth to know who had been on the phone and what had been said. Zigzagging through the crowded corridor and across the large, square booking area, he slipped into a tall revolving door and hissed out into the heat.

The sound of Manila immediately attacked him. The traffic seemed endless and immobile. Judging by the din, a permanent blaring of the horn was a Filipino license requirement. He bounced down the steps two at a time and joined a queue at the nearest cabstand.

Three people were ahead of him, and he waited patiently, turning back to look at the tall, vacant face of the police station. For a moment he had the suspicion that someone inside was watching him, but he shrugged it off. He was exhausted and he needed time to think.

It seemed almost too perfectly coincidental that Charles Harding would be present in the airport during a terrorist attack. The odds argued strongly that it had not been a freak occurrence. If Harding had been the target, who had done the shooting? And why there? But Bolan couldn't come up with a single reason why anyone should go to such trouble to try to kill one man when he could just as easily be taken out some other way, someplace safer for the shooters.

Unless, Bolan thought...unless it had to look like a fluke to hide the purpose, and possibly the people, behind it. Collazo had told him virtually nothing about the attack. He didn't even know whether anyone had been killed. But even if there had been fatalities, Bolan knew enough about the world to understand that incidental death raised no eyebrows in the pursuit of political goals.

Not anymore.

A cab finally arrived, and all three people in front of him piled into it. Bolan didn't have long to wait for the next one. He gave the driver his destination, then settled back in the seat. He hadn't been to the Philippines in so long, and yet it seemed the same. The people were a little happier with Marcos gone, but it seemed like a happiness that was only skin-deep. Everyplace he looked, he saw a guardedness, like trespassers walking through a graveyard at midnight. The peace was fragile, they seemed to say, as fragile as the eggs they all walked on.

And, like most Third World countries, it was a place where Americans were barely tolerated, at least by a highly vocal minority. Nobody likes a cop, Bolan thought, and when you're the world's cop, nobody on earth really likes you. They want you to be there when they need help, but they don't want to feel grateful for it.

Bolan watched the traffic slide by as the driver twirled the steering wheel, maneuvering the cab as if it were as thin as a knife blade. He darted through narrow openings without braking, sometimes gunning the engine for an extra burst of speed. The streets teemed with pedestrians, and in some respects it looked no different from any other major capital. Westernized to a fault, the residents looked as if they would have been equally at home in downtown New York or the streets of Singapore.

But there was another Manila, another Philippines. Most Westerners rarely saw it, if at all. It was the Manila of rusting corrugated metal shacks and strings of shanties made of packing crates and tarpaper. This was the Manila that Marcos had made a career of ignoring, and Aquino had built a career making promises to. If any of those promises had been kept, it was a closely held secret.

Not that Aquino was entirely to blame. You don't hold one person responsible for centuries of misery. But the forgotten people were still there, packed into their slums like gunpowder, just waiting for the spark. He wondered if the attack at the airport was the overture of a new rebellion, one to make the New People's Army look like Boy Scouts and the Huks like pacific idealists. The potential was there—that was a certainty.

In the back of Bolan's mind was the faint glimmer, dim as a penlight at the bottom of a mine shaft, that Charles Harding had come with the same notion, maybe to set that spark or maybe to piss on it and put it out. But Harding's background, sketchy as it was, suggested that he was not a disinterested observer in the Filipino political process. It was here, after all, that Lansdale had cut his eyeteeth, honing those theories that had gone so badly astray in Vietnam.

The cab suddenly swerved to the left and rocked to a halt. Bolan looked out at the ultramodern glass-and-brass facade of the MacArthur Hilton. He paid the hack, then eased out of the cab. The clean pavement, flecked with glittering flakes of mica catching the sun, looked as if it had just been laid. He pushed through the revolving door as the cab lurched away, leaving the scent of burnt rubber hanging in the humid air.

Bolan checked in quickly, and was surprised when the clerk said that someone had been asking for him. Bolan waited, watching the clerk curiously. He expected one of those ubiquitous pink papers with a phone message scribbled on it, but was instead surprised to hear the clerk page Frank Henson.

He turned to see a man in a rumpled suit making a beeline for the desk. It had to be Henson.

"Now what?" Bolan muttered.

5

Frank Henson slipped behind the wheel of his Land Rover and leaned across to open Bolan's door. The big guy climbed in and dropped his bag over the seat into the back.

"They give you a hard time today?" Henson asked.

"I've had worse."

"They say anything about Harding?"

"Collazo referred to him obliquely, but didn't really give much away. I don't know what he knows, but I don't think it's much. It was more like he was trying to pump me than anything else."

Henson laughed easily. "Son of a bitch! I'd love to know where the holes are. We're leaking like a sieve. And everybody in Manila seems to know what we know before we know it. Guy I bought this rattletrap from, some damn assistant something or other at the British embassy, told me about Harding two days before I heard his name from anybody else."

"You think it's on your end or back in D.C.?" Bolan watched Henson carefully while the older man composed his answer. It would be easy to blame it on the other guy. That was the way in any bureaucracy.

"I wish to Christ I knew," Henson said, laughing again. "I'd like to blame it on Washington. Those bastards are always looking for something to talk about at their cocktail parties. But I just don't know."

Bolan made a mental note to be circumspect in his dealing with Henson. It wasn't that he didn't trust the man, but if there was a leak in Manila, it could get him killed. In the back of his mind was the not so sneaking suspicion that the airport scene had not been a coincidence. He also had to consider the possibility that he himself had been the target.

Henson negotiated the traffic with a casual hand, flowing with it rather than trying to outrun it. Like most Far Eastern capitals, it combined the slowest of traditional commerce with the frenzy of blaring horns.

"I think we can talk more freely at my place," Henson said. "I have it swept a couple of times a week. Had it done this afternoon, as a matter of fact."

"I'm beginning to think this thing is a lot more complicated than Walt Wilson told me."

"That's Rosebud for you. Walt's a crackerjack, but he's never liked to tell a guy more than he has to. In this case, I think, probably even less."

"Tell me what you know about Charles Harding."

"First off, Harding's just the tip of the iceberg. I don't know where the hell he gets his money, but he's got backing, big backing."

"But what does he do here?"

"What I know, or what I think?"

"Both."

"I know he fronts some sort of political action organization out in the boondocks. They're on some sort of paramilitary trip. They got more guns than the NPA, more money than you can shake a stick at, and they are plugged into the Philippine Army six ways to Sunday. There's a dozen laws, at least, against what he's doing, but he's never even gotten a parking ticket, so far as I know."

"What sort of politics?"

"I know what you're asking and, no, no way he's a Communist front. If you know anything at all about the guy, you know he's out there on the fringe, somewhere between Tricky Dick and Attila. No, that's the puzzle, really. I mean, most of these right-wing diehards sit home running beer companies and shit. They send money, but they don't put their asses on the line. Harding's different. He's out there with the grunts. Except nobody really knows where *there* is." Henson rapped on the horn to nudge a particularly slow-moving truck along. "And that, my friend, brings us to the end of what I know."

"What about what you think?"

"Ah...what I think...that's something altogether different. That is very scary stuff indeed."

Bolan waited patiently while Henson thought about how to begin.

Finally Henson cleared his throat. "Okay, here's what I think. I think Mr. Harding is a madman. I think he wants to see Cory take a pratfall and lay there in the mud with her skirt up around her hips. I think he is working for that very thing, and I think he will stop at nothing, including provoking a civil war, to get it done."

"What's the percentage?"

"Hey, am I a madman? How the fuck should I know? He's one of these guys looks under his bed every night, and not just to see if the maid did the floor. You know what I mean?"

"Still, why here?"

"Why here? That's an easy one. Charlie-boy did his time in Southeast Asia. He's a domino player from the old school. You look at a map of the Pacific, and what do you see? Who controls it? From Hawaii on to India, the Philippines is basically what we got. You lose Subic, you're stuck with Australia and New Zealand, and neither one of them wants nukes in port on three-day leave. That creates a power vacuum in the Pacific basin. And not just for Mr. Charles Harding, either."

"So you think he wants to install a government that will let us keep Clark and Subic? Is that it?"

"That's part of it. Part of it's some weird megalomania, though. I think he thrives on chaos. There's been a gradually escalating terror campaign in the big cities, especially Manila. I'm convinced he's behind it, but I can't prove it. And I'll tell you something else. If anybody's running him, he's got his hands full. There is no way in hell to control this guy. He's too flaky. I'd rather play football with a bottle of nitroglycerin than try to ride herd on Harding."

"Where's the NPA fit in?"

"Good question. I've been getting reports that they're suffering heavy losses in the mountains. But there hasn't been any significant army action up there in months. Aquino has too much else to worry about. They go on punitive expeditions if there's been a serious assault by the NPA, but there hasn't been one that amounted to anything since last year."

"You think Harding's behind it?"

"Who else? The NPA might be amateurs, but they don't shoot one another. Not that often, anyhow."

Henson lapsed into silence, as if the conversation had drained him. He drove like a robot, his eyes staring straight ahead through the bug-splattered glass. They were on the edge of the city, and the broad avenues gradually spilled into narrow, tree-lined streets. Tropical lushness was everywhere. Most of the houses were all but hidden behind masses of bougainvillea and something that looked like rhododendron. Few lights broke the darkness, and many of them did little more than dart in and out among the leaves as the evening breeze whipped the overhanging branches around.

Henson started to whistle between his teeth, and Bolan watched him curiously. He seemed on edge, as if there were something he wanted to say, but didn't quite know how to phrase.

"Anything wrong?" Bolan asked, trying to prompt him.

Henson sucked his teeth for a few seconds. "I don't know. I'm arguing with myself. I don't...ah, what the hell..." He slapped the wheel with the heel of his right hand. "I've been working on a pipeline for a few months. I was just thinking, maybe, if I could hook you up, maybe it would get us somewhere. I just don't know."

"What kind of pipeline?"

"An odd duck, a guy named Colgan. If Harding is a mad bomber, and there's no doubt in my mind he is, then this guy's the mad hatter. He's a doctor—he runs these clinics. He thinks he's the third way, or something like that. It's all mystical gobbledygook, but he believes it and he's got people who believe it right along with him. I'll tell you about it when we get to my place. Another five minutes. Let me chew on it...."

Bolan stared out the window, watching the trees go by. The homes were few and far between now. He wondered why Henson had chosen to live so far out of the city. It seemed odd, almost as if Henson were trying to isolate himself from the people he was supposed to understand.

Henson turned the wheel sharply, and the high-riding Rover leaned uncomfortably as they turned into a narrow side street.

"It's at the end of the block," Henson said. "My little hermitage of sorts. Sometimes I think I've been at this business too long. I'm under diplomatic cover, and the ambassador keeps leaning on me to move into Manila, but I can't stand the thought of it. This place can break your heart, Bolan. It's so beautiful you can hardly believe it, but then when you see how the people live, it looks like hell on earth. I've seen enough of that, Laos in particular, in the late sixties. I just can't take it anymore. I got another year, and then I'm out of it."

Bolan opened his mouth to respond when the Rover bounced over a pothole. His teeth clacked together. Henson began to swerve back and forth, slaloming the blocky

Rover down a pitted lane. A small house materialized in the headlights a hundred yards ahead.

"There it is," Henson said, "home, sweet home."

He gunned the Rover, then let it coast the rest of the way, braking just as it rolled past the steps to a small side porch. Henson jumped out almost eagerly, as though the place really were some sort of refuge.

"Wait here," he said. "I'll go in the front door and let you in right here."

He sprinted back toward the front of the house. Bolan heard a door slam, then watched as a succession of lights appeared in the windows as Henson made his way toward the rear. A moment later the door opened in front of him, and Henson stepped back with a bow. "Welcome," he said.

Bolan climbed the two steps and found himself in a small kitchen. Henson immediately turned and disappeared through another door. "Come on in and sit down," he shouted over his shoulder.

Bolan followed. The first room was a small library, its shelves bulging with the pale blue and green paper bindings of government reports as well as a healthy sampling of more usual volumes in cloth and paper. The next room was twice as large. Bolan immediately noticed the walls.

Henson caught his eye, and said, "Rubbings . . . my wife, ex-wife actually, taught me how to do them. She was an art student when I met her. We used to practice on old gravestones in Philadelphia. These are mine, though, from every place I've been. Temples from Laos and Burma, mostly, but one or two from every stop I've made on my somewhat circuitous transit through the typical State Department itinerary."

He grabbed a stack of magazines from a chair and pointed. "Have a seat. I'll get us something cold."

Bolan sank into the chair gratefully. It was nice to sit on something that wasn't moving. He glanced at one of the rubbings as Henson called, "Beer okay? It's Japanese, but it's cold."

"Fine," Bolan shouted back.

The refrigerator door banged back with a rattle of bottles in its shelves. The next thing he heard sounded like Armageddon. The blast momentarily deafened him. Smoke boiled through the doorway as he jumped to his feet.

"Henson," he called. "Frank, what . . ."

He covered his mouth with a forearm and charged into the library. It was full of smoke and plaster dust so thick he couldn't see. He ducked down to try to get under the worst of it, but did no better. The doorway to the kitchen was blocked with debris. He grabbed a piece of timber with both hands and tugged but couldn't dislodge anything. The dust was choking him as he backed away a step, then sprinted for the front door.

He leapt from the front porch and careered around the corner, where he stopped in disbelief. The whole rear half of the side wall lay splattered across the lawn. Several beams jutted up at an angle where they had smashed into the roof of the Rover.

Bolan climbed up onto the rear bumper and hauled himself into the wreckage. There wasn't a chance in hell Frank Henson had survived the blast, but he had to be sure. The ruined wall shifted under his weight. The whole room still boiled with swirling clouds of dust.

Bolan realized the bomb must have been in the refrigerator, primed to detonate when the door was opened. He could just make out the ruined hulk, shaped like a bulging barrel, its top split and twisted into modern art.

"Henson," he shouted. "Henson?"

There was no answer. And as the dust began to settle, he knew there wouldn't be. Frank Henson had been splattered all over the kitchen. The settling dust began to crust on the bloodstains, hiding the bright smears with an orangy film.

But he could still see where they were.

6

Bolan closed the door quickly. His eyes scanned the interior, and nothing looked out of place. But that didn't mean a thing. He knew that if they had gotten to Henson, they could get to him.

Breathing in slowly, holding it until his lungs were close to bursting, he checked the room carefully, his Desert Eagle at the ready. He peered in every conceivable place, from under the bed for a pressure switch to the medicine cabinet for a spring release. When he had looked everywhere, he relaxed. He needed to free his mind so he could consider the situation at hand.

Cautiously he sat on the bed and examined the envelope. His name had been scrawled across it in black Magic Marker. The plain white envelope had been sealed with cellophane tape. It contained four sheets of paper. One was a grainy picture, apparently a Xerox of an old newspaper photograph, of Charles Harding. The second was a story, headline and all, about the incident at the airport. He scanned the story quickly, stopping at the underlined words, "an unknown American." Backing up, he read the entire paragraph and realized the phrase applied to him. There was no other mark on the page, just that short, thin line under the three words.

The third sheet was a map, roughly drawn in blue pencil, of Ongpin, Manila's Chinatown. The map was highlighted by a single red dot at the intersection of Rizal and Santa

Margarita. The last paper was a sheet of cheap typing paper. In the same hand as that on the envelope, the words "If you have to ask, you'll never know" had been scrawled with the same Magic Marker. Underneath the inscription were the typewritten words, "twelve midnight."

Bolan was mystified. Apparently someone wanted to meet him, someone who knew he had been at the airport that afternoon, and who also knew of his interest in Charles Harding. But who?

His head hurt and he couldn't think straight. He needed some rest, but there was no time. He glanced at the clock radio next to the bed. It read 11:17 in sickly green digits. He had less than an hour. He debated whether or not to keep the appointment, but it was no contest. Not really. There was no way in hell he could afford to pass up the invitation, and he knew it.

Cursing Walt Wilson for getting him into such a mess, he splashed cold water on his face and strapped on a second harness, this one for the Beretta. Stuffing a couple of extra clips into his coat pocket, one for each weapon, he stared at himself in the huge round mirror over the dresser. He looked exhausted, but was used to that. He also looked confused, and that was cause for concern. He was not accustomed to standing on such shifting sand. As if it hadn't been bad enough to travel halfway around the world on the tail of a man about whom he knew next to nothing, he was now slated to meet someone unknown, who apparently knew a great deal about him.

He kept thinking back to Walt Wilson. Henson had hinted that there was more to the picture than Wilson had given him. His own suspicions were simmering beneath the surface, but he had nothing to cool them or to bring them to a boil, either. Something wasn't right, and he couldn't avoid the suspicion that he'd been sent into a minefield wearing cast-iron shoes and a blindfold.

Slipping into his jacket again, tugging it down to fit comfortably over the artillery, he headed for the door. As he reached for the doorknob, it turned. The motion had been slight, no more than a fraction of an inch or so, but genuine. He reached under his coat for the Desert Eagle and flattened himself against the wall.

He stared at the knob for a long minute, but it didn't move again. Straining his ears, Bolan listened for the slightest sound out in the carpeted hall. He thought he heard footsteps, but the sound vanished almost as soon as it registered. He muffled the latch with one palm and turned the lock. Jerking the door wide open, he checked one end of the hall, the Desert Eagle held against his right ear. Switching sides, dropping the gun to belt level, he checked the other end of the hall. It, too, was empty. Cautiously he stuck his head out to make sure, but the hall was absolutely quiet. He took a tentative step into the corridor.

He heard a snick behind him and spun around just as the fire door at the end of the hall closed. Sprinting on the thick carpet, he raced to the fire door and pressed an ear against it. He heard footsteps on the stairs and ripped the door open. The steps continued on down, and Bolan plunged into the stairwell just as another door, several floors below, banged shut.

Bolan took the stairs two at a time, knowing even as he raced down the second flight that he was too late. It wasn't possible to guess which door had slammed. Rather than waste time in a pointless search, he continued on down to the ground floor. Slipping the Desert Eagle under his jacket, he stepped into the lobby. It, too, was empty, except for a clerk behind the bell desk, absorbed in a newspaper.

Outside, the traffic was still fairly heavy, considering the hour, and Bolan checked his watch as he headed for the door. Out in the muggy night, he spotted a cab at once and jumped in, giving the driver his destination even before closing the door. The cabby jerked the lever on his meter and swung away from the curb as Bolan slammed the door.

Without warning, the driver made a U-turn, to the amusement of a traffic cop who was sitting sidesaddle on a Honda scooter. The cabby waved, and the cop waved back. "My brother-in-law," the cabby explained.

Weaving expertly through the tangled traffic, the cabdriver threaded needle after needle. Gradually, as they moved away from the heart of downtown Manila, the only part of the city Western tourists cared to see after dark, the traffic thinned and its character changed. Instead of taxi cabs and fancy limousines, rolling collections of dents and rusted fenders began to predominate. Battered cars, vans and assorted commercial delivery trucks flowed steadily past, like the brown waters of a river slipping by the gunwales of a launch headed upstream.

"Got to make deliveries at night. Too much traffic in the daytime," the driver said without taking his eyes off the road.

Bolan was not in the mood for idle chatter, so he said nothing. The driver seemed to sense his mood, and set his jaw. At the appropriate corner, he pulled over to the edge of the walkway and announced the fare. Bolan paid him and slipped out on the street side.

He had thought it best to cover the last couple of blocks on foot. He'd been set up too often in the past to get careless and make it easy for the other side. The street was lined with shops on both sides, all bearing signs in Chinese ideograms and some also in English. Every window was dark. As he walked past, Bolan's eye caught the whole panoply of Far Eastern trade. Silks and ivory carvings, firecrackers and Japanese cameras, imported foods and homegrown crafts were piled helter-skelter in bins behind every pane of glass.

Twice he hesitated before crossing the mouth of a dark alley. The street was surprisingly clean. He could just imagine the jungle the street would become in five or six hours, and marveled that not a single scrap of paper stirred in the slight, sticky breeze. Crossing a narrow side street, Bolan glanced in both directions, but saw nothing out of the ordinary. A striped cat darting in among the silent vans was the only living thing he saw.

Entering the last block, he wondered where he was supposed to go. All four corners were dark. He slowed his pace a little more, listening intently for the slightest sound. There was only the grinding of sand on the asphalt underfoot. Halfway down the block, he stopped and ducked into a doorway. His watch read 11:53. He scanned the two corner buildings on the opposite side of the street, but both were dark and closed up tight. Not even a window open to catch a little of the breeze broke the seamless face of either building.

Puzzled, he crossed the street and ducked into another doorway. He had the Desert Eagle in his hand now. He didn't like the quiet. He didn't like the darkness, either. The quiet seemed almost palpable, too perfect and too absolute. It reminded him of countless western streets—Dodge City, Abilene, Tombstone—in too many western movies. It was the calm before the final shootout, when every window was closed, and somebody peered into the silent street from behind every curtain.

He had the urge to shake things up. His eyes bored into the second pair of corner buildings, each as dark and silent as the other two.

He was getting close to that antsy frustration that assaulted him whenever things were totally out of control. It was as if someone had handed him a perfectly smooth globe of polished obsidian and said, "Here, open it."

In the unnatural quiet Bolan could hear his heart, its rhythm throbbing in his ears. He stared at the shop on the near corner. The English portion of its sign read "Fabrick," but he didn't smile at the misspelling. Like everything else, it just seemed one more proof that things were out of whack.

He started to look away when something caught his eye. He riveted his gaze on the spot where it had been, but there was nothing there. It had been, or at least he thought it had been, a brief flicker, as if a candle had passed by or a match been struck and extinguished. Then again. It flashed, and he was certain this time.

He waited, aware that he was holding his breath, as if to exhale would kill the delicate glimmer behind the dusty glass. It had become steady, electric light rather than a flame, but it did nothing. Losing his patience, Bolan began to fidget in the doorway. When the light disappeared again, he sprinted across the street at an angle. Pressing his face to the glass, he tried to see inside, past the cascading silks. They tumbled over a rack in thick, almost seamless folds.

He tapped on the window with his knuckles, and the glass rattled in its peeling wooden frame. A chunk of putty fell from the bottom of the pane and hit his foot. He backed away from the glass to look down. He started to lean back in when he saw something behind him, reflected in the glass. He began to turn as the gray blur dissolved. He was halfway around when the window, now almost behind him, cracked.

Instinctively he fell to the ground. He looked for cover, but there was none to be had. He started to move, crab-walking under the window ledge to the corner, when something slammed into the wooden wall just above his head.

At the corner he scurried across the rounded concrete step and ducked in behind the far wall. Desperately he scanned the silent row of shops across the street. The gray blur he had seen was gone. In all probability, it had been the gunman. Cautiously he got to his knees, straining to see through the dark glass across the street.

The next shot tore a chunk of wood from the window frame just above his shoulder. Sharp splinters stabbed his left cheek, and he dropped to the ground again. He still didn't know where the shots had come from. The gun was silenced, and there hadn't been a flash, either.

Then he saw the gunman, just a block of dark gray in the mouth of an alley four shops from the corner. Inching forward, Bolan rested the muzzle of the Desert Eagle on the six-inch step. The shooter was being careful. He didn't leave much exposed. Bolan was about to squeeze the trigger when a second shadow moved, then a third.

Shifting his aim, he drew a bead on the nearest shadow, just a blob of darkness on the roof, blotting out a few stars. As he squeezed, the shadow opened up. Unfolding like a leaf, it stood erect and let loose with a burst of suppressed fire. The slugs chewed at the corner of the building, sparking where they hit the concrete, and Bolan cringed against the wall. When the firing stopped, he ducked back out and squeezed off two quick shots. The shadow on the roof folded back into itself, then toppled over the edge and landed with a dull thud on the pavement.

Bolan ducked back and took a deep breath. There had been at least four shooters. They were one shy now, but that was cold comfort.

In the street behind him, a dull roar exploded into thunder. He turned to see where it came from just as another burst of lead clawed at the pavement in front of him. A blocky shadow hurtled toward him, its engine whining. It was a dark-colored van, one set of wheels on the curb the other still on the street.

Bolan scrambled to his feet. Emptying the Desert Eagle at the far side of the street, he squeezed into the doorway and smashed the window glass with his elbow. Diving through the shattered frame of the door, he landed heavily on his shoulder. The window to his left blew out, and a steady hail of fire chewed the window display to tatters. Bolan pressed himself against the wooden floor.

The van squealed to a halt outside as Bolan reloaded with quick and practiced hands. He looked over his shoulder to see the van parked across the doorway, blocking his way out.

The van's passenger door swung open, and another metallic slam, probably its rear doors, echoed inside the shattered shop. Bolan drew the AutoMag and started to back away from the broken window. He bumped into something he couldn't see in the dark and fell backward just as the shop's second window caved inward. The roar of cascading glass died away into a tinkle that was almost playful, like a windup music box.

As he struggled to regain his feet among the tangled bolts of cloth, he felt a hand on his shoulder.

"Come this way. Quickly!"

It was a woman's voice, but he could see nothing in the pitch-black shop. She tugged again on his arm, and he followed her, stumbling twice as an assassin tumbled through the broken window and swept the darkness with an automatic rifle.

7

Bolan nearly knocked the woman down when she stopped suddenly. In a hoarse whisper, she told him to back up a step, and he heard a bolt being thrown. The squeak of metal hinges let him know she was opening a door, then she was pulling on his arm again. He banged his head on a hard surface, probably the door frame, and he staggered drunkenly until she pushed him against a wall by placing both palms flat against his chest.

"Don't move," she whispered. Her voice seemed to come from below his chest. He guessed she couldn't be any more than five two or five three.

The dull thud of footsteps pounded back in the direction they had come. He heard the hinges squeak again, and shouted voices that seemed to be swallowed by the darkness as the door swung closed.

For the third time her hand snatched at his sleeve, and again he followed her, bending low to avoid another crack in his skull. His head throbbed from the previous collision, and every step seemed to split the bone a little wider. He rubbed his forehead just below the hairline and found a lump the size of a robin's egg. His fingers came away sticky.

They rattled down a stairwell, the woman pulling him like an angry mother dragging along a wayward child.

He wanted to ask where they were going, but her pace was picking up and he had to concentrate on keeping up with her. Running in the darkness, he felt as if he couldn't breathe. He was getting tense, wary of slamming into another obstacle he couldn't see, and the anxiety helped to drain his reserves of energy.

Reaching out with one hand, he brushed his fingertips against what seemed to be a rock wall, likely raw stone cut into rough blocks. Dampness trickled down over the stone, and something soft, probably moss, filled the seams. He still hadn't seen a glimmer of light, and marveled at the woman's ability to move so quickly in such impenetrable blackness.

They were far enough away from the shop that he could hear nothing but his feet on damp earth, his steps drowning out those of the woman ahead of him. His throat felt raw, and his breathing rasped in his ears like a swarm of flies. His mouth was dry, and it felt as if his tongue were growing thick between his teeth.

Just when he was about to call for a break, she began to slow down, and he stumbled to a halt. He leaned over and breathed deeply.

"Where are we?" Bolan asked.

"Does it matter?" she responded.

"You've got a point," Bolan said. "Will you at least tell me who you are?"

"You don't need to know that, either. Not yet."

"You're a regular gold mine of information," Bolan commented.

She ignored the sarcasm. "When you need to know, you will know. But not before."

She stepped close to him and hissed, "Shhh!" Even though he couldn't see her in the darkness, he knew she was suddenly straining to hear something.

Bolan held his breath. He, too, thought he could hear something. It was distant and muffled. It came from some distance behind them, but he couldn't tell whether it was all the way back at the shop or closer.

"What is it?" he whispered.

"I'm not sure. But we'd better go."

Bolan nodded. Then, realizing she couldn't see him, he whispered, "Okay."

Again she reached out to grab his arm, but the tugging was more gentle, as if finally satisfied that he would follow her lead without argument.

They had gone no more than fifty feet when she slowed again.

"What's wrong?" he asked.

"Nothing. There is a door here. Wait while I open it."

He stood stock-still, listening to her work a latch in the darkness. There was no fumbling. It was almost as though her fingers had eyes. Smoothly the lock opened, and she pulled the door back. "Go on," she prompted.

Bolan brushed against her as he stepped through the door. He stopped on the other side and waited for her to close and relock the door. A thunderclap echoed through the darkness, and Bolan heard her gasp.

"They broke through," she said. "We must hurry." The words were no sooner out of her mouth than a wall of air slammed into them. The concussion knocked her to the floor, and Bolan heard her moan. He knelt on one knee and groped for her in the darkness. His fingers found rough cloth. It felt like denim, and he let his hand follow the seam of her pants to her hip. Her hand closed over his.

"Help me up," she said. "I have to close the door."

"Are you all right?"

"Never mind, just help me up." She pulled on his arm, trying to haul herself to her feet.

"It's easier for me," he said. He yanked her up, apologizing for his roughness. She ignored him, and he could hear the whisper of her fingers on the damp stone as she looked for the door frame. Thudding feet sounded far down the passage, and the shouted commands, distorted by the distance and the narrow tunnel, blurred into a meaningless babble.

He was about to offer his help again when he heard the hinges squeal, and the heavy door slammed shut, blocking out the approaching thudding of booted feet.

"Don't you have a light?" he asked as she threw a heavy bolt home. Before she answered, he heard two heavy thumps. He realized she must have been dropping bars into place across the inside of the door.

"I don't need a light," she said. "Come on."

She slipped past him, her body brushing against him in the narrow passage. Once more he felt her hand close over his wrist, and she pulled him along after her.

Bolan could tell by the unevenness of her stride that she had been hurt by the fall. She seemed to be limping. Far ahead, like some geometric hologram, a rectangle of brilliant lines began to glow. It grew larger as they ran, and Bolan realized they were approaching another door, beyond which there was light.

"Not much farther," she said through teeth clenched against the pain.

Bolan could tell when to stop, and he waited impatiently while she fumbled with the door. It swung open without warning, and the surge of white light hurt his eyes. He turned away, squinting to protect his eyes, and barely avoided tripping down a pair of steps.

Behind him, she slammed the door, rammed the last bar in place and turned to him. Her lips were set in a straight line. Her face was as nearly expressionless as any face he'd ever seen. "Now that we can see again, you can go back to feeling superior," she said. "You can lead the way."

She stretched out a bronze hand, her long, delicate fingers quivering like the fronds of a water plant swaying in the current. Bolan closed his huge hand over hers and patted her on his forearm. "You tell me where to go," he said.

"Don't tempt me," she stated. She shook her head slightly, then pointed to the wall behind him. "Through that door."

"Are you willing to talk to me now?"

"Nothing has changed," she said. Her lips returned to their rigid set as Bolan scrutinized her. He had been right about her height—if anything, perhaps an inch too generous. Her hair was as black as the tunnel they'd just left behind, and was piled on her head and held in place with simple combs of ivory or bone. An exquisite face hovered under the jet-black cloud like a coppery mist, broken only by a hint of pale lipstick. She wore jeans and a green work shirt, neither of which did much to conceal the generous figure.

"You're lovely," he said matter-of-factly, surprised that the words had come out of his mouth. Despite her seeming toughness, there was something innocent about her.

But she misunderstood. "And you're wasting time," she said with just the suggestion of a smile.

Not bothering to explain, Bolan shrugged before turning slowly. She moved after him, her hand resting lightly on his shoulder now. He opened the door she had pointed out and stepped through.

"No need to lock this one," she said as she followed him into the next room.

"Where to now?"

"Straight ahead."

Bolan nodded, then said, "All right."

They were in a large, empty room. Its ceiling was thirty feet above them, composed of corrugated tin over rusting girders. It appeared to have functioned as a warehouse at one time.

"Go all the way across," she prompted.

"Don't we have to worry about them blowing through the other doors, just like they did the first?"

"That's been taken care of," she said.

He didn't know whether she meant it to sound cryptic, but it had that effect.

As they neared the center of the huge room, her hand slapped him on the shoulder. He stopped, thinking he had been going too fast. He turned to wait for her, and realized she was deliberately backing away from him.

"What's the matter?" Bolan asked.

She shook her head. "Nothing."

He took a step toward her, but she held up a hand. "Stay right there," she hissed.

He heard a rustling sound and turned toward it. Four men, each carrying an automatic rifle that was trained on his midsection, stood in a semicircle.

"You are in no danger," she assured him. "I'm sorry, but it has to be this way. You will understand soon."

At a gesture from one of the men, Bolan raised his hands. He thought, for one fleeting instant, about reaching for the AutoMag. But it was hopeless. They would cut him in half before he got his hand on the butt of the big .44.

They stood there in a motionless tableau for a long moment. Bolan examined the men in turn, and shook his head. They were cut from the same cloth. All small, wiry and dressed in faded GI camous. The only way to tell them apart was by the four different mustaches.

One of the men split off from the others and advanced on Bolan from the right side. He kept his rifle, an AK-47, at the ready until he slipped in behind Bolan. Quickly the Desert Eagle and the Beretta were lifted. The man knelt for a moment to pat him down. When he was satisfied, he tugged Bolan's hands down behind him and clicked a pair of handcuffs in place.

"Too tight?" the man asked.

"Not if I have to wear them at all," Bolan said.

"Sorry, Señor Belasko. But we have to take precautions. We mean you no harm. You will see."

Bolan flinched when the blindfold was looped over his head. It happened so suddenly that he thought the man meant to garrote him, and sighed when the cloth was positioned over his eyes.

"Who the hell are you people?" Bolan demanded.

"All in good time, Mr. Belasko. Please, be patient." It was the woman who spoke.

He felt her hand on his arm again. She simply squeezed reassuringly, then let her hand fall away. Bolan heard a heavy door rolling on a metal track, and the rumble of an engine. It sounded like a van or small truck. He thought immediately of the van that had charged him from the rear, and wondered whether it was the same one. Then, realizing that under the circumstances it didn't much matter, he pushed the thought out of his mind.

The vehicle approached, stopped nearly in front of him, and hands pushed him forward.

"Step up, a little higher," one of the men said. He was helped into the van and heard a door close. He sensed someone present and, as if in answer to his unspoken question, the woman said, "Don't worry. You are not alone."

Not much, Bolan thought.

8

Bolan tried to plot the course of the truck in his head. He quickly gave it up when he realized he had no idea of his starting point. They had run so far and so long in the tunnel that the warehouse could have been anywhere. And because of the motion of the truck, it was impossible to gauge direction from inside. The truck rocked and rolled heavily, making it difficult to tell when they turned and when they had merely rolled through a particularly large pothole or around an obstacle in the road.

He had tried to engage the woman in conversation, but each time, she turned him away with a single syllable. After the third time, he gave up. If she had anything to say to him, she would say it, he decided. So far she hadn't.

They had been traveling for nearly two hours, and his shoulders were sore from slamming into the sides of the van. No matter how he positioned himself, a sudden jolt would dislodge him and send him pounding into a steel wall or tilt him over onto the floor.

Finally he lay flat, wedging himself into a corner, and let gravity do what it could to protect him. With his hands cuffed behind him, it was far from comfortable, but at least he would spare himself the worst of the bumps and bruises.

Resigning himself to his situation, he tried to sleep but found, paradoxically, that it was too dark. He thought of what it was like to lie in bed and watch the play of light and shadow on the ceiling: the glare of passing headlights, the gradual passage of the moon, the winking blue or red of neon outside a cheap hotel window, all the things that conspired to prevent the darkness of the night from being perfect.

He sighed in exasperation, and she must have realized what he was thinking. "There is nothing quite like it, you know."

"Like what?" Bolan asked.

"Like being hostage to someone's whim, simply because he has a gun...."

"I'm sure," Bolan replied, not knowing what else to say, but feeling the need to say something to keep her talking.

"I'm almost used to it." Her voice sounded uncertain. It echoed hollowly off the walls of the van. "No, I'm not, actually. I don't know why I always say that."

"Maybe that's the only way you can deal with it."

"I suppose."

"How long have you carried a gun?"

"A year. Almost..."

"What drove you to it?"

"Never mind. I don't want to talk about it." She lapsed into a silence that sounded as if it were meant to be permanent.

They rode without speaking for a quarter of an hour. Bolan found himself trying to visualize her. It had been just a few hours since he'd seen her, but he was unable to do it. Her face kept drifting in and out of focus. It hovered there, just beyond the reach of his mind, fluttering like a phony ghost at Halloween. Every time he pushed toward it, it slipped away, teasing him with its impermanence.

When the silence was broken again, it was she who broke it. "What is Charles Harding to you?" Her voice was so soft, he wasn't sure he had understood the question.

"Did you say something?" he asked.

"I asked you what Charles Harding was to you." She snapped it precisely this time.

"Right now, a question mark in an empty box. Why?"

"You tried to help him at the airport. I was just wondering why, that's all."

"Actually I wasn't. If I was trying to help anybody, it was a thousand innocent people who were walking into the middle of a terrorist attack."

"I don't believe that, you know. I just don't."

"Believe what you want."

"You really should tell me."

"Why should I tell you anything? You know my name and I don't know yours. You know a lot more about me than I do about you. And I'm not in the habit of sharing my life story with total strangers, kidnappers or not."

"You're not being kidnapped. Don't be so melodramatic."

"What do you call it?"

"What difference does it make what I call it? Labels don't mean anything, anyway. And my name is Marisa."

The truck hit a particularly rough bump, and he landed hard on his tailbone as the truck bed twisted and bounced. Bolan groaned and wriggled around to lie on his side.

"Are you all right?" she asked.

"I've been better."

"I'm used to it, I guess. Lying in a truck in the dark, I mean. I can control my body. It's almost as if I know where the bumps are before we hit them."

"Bully for you."

"Don't be bitter."

"Whatever you say." Bolan's jaw slammed shut like a mausoleum door.

He heard her shift position, and a moment later he felt her hands groping past his hip. He didn't know what she was after until the handcuffs clicked.

"I really shouldn't have done that...."

"I'll never tell," Bolan said.

"No, I mean it. You have to promise you won't try to get away."

"I'm not about to jump out of a speeding truck in the middle of the night, if that's what you mean. Other than that, I'm not making any promises."

"I have a gun, you know."

He reached up to take off the blindfold.

"What do you mean?" She seemed genuinely puzzled. She levered a shell into the chamber of an automatic pistol, and Bolan didn't need to see her to know it.

"Look, I . . ." He stumbled to a halt. It seemed as if he couldn't say anything without tripping all over himself. There was something about her that mystified him.

"Funny, isn't it, how much we take power for granted? I mean, we refer to it constantly. We use it interchangeably with privilege as if they were the same thing." She seemed completely unruffled. Her voice was serene, almost narcotized, and nearly hypnotic. "But they aren't the same thing at all. Right now, I have a kind of power that you don't. That makes me privileged, compared to you."

"How so?"

"If I say jump, you will ask how high. All because I have the gun."

"Maybe. Maybe not."

She ignored the implicit disagreement. "But that's not all. It makes us different, having power. It also puts you on the defensive, the same way knowledge does. Knowledge, too, is a kind of power."

"You think so?"

"I know it. Take the fact that you really don't know why you're here. Not the truck—I don't mean that. I mean Manila. The Philippines. I think maybe that's why I took off your handcuffs. You are a kind of innocent. You're like a child, somehow. Most things are so simple for you, and yet some things are so complex you don't even try to understand them. But you don't care. For you, they amount to the same thing. You see something in black and white, or you don't see it at all. And you don't even realize that."

Bolan listened to the laboring engine for a while. He could feel it throbbing through the floorboards. From the strain, and the slight imbalance he felt, he assumed they were heading uphill now, and had been for a while. Slowly, perhaps, but certainly.

Finally he took up the gauntlet. "If you understand so much, why don't you explain things to me? Show me where I am wrong and you are right."

"You think I can't, don't you?"

"I don't think anything. Just do it, if you can."

"All right...let me tell you about your Mr. Charles Harding. How about that for a beginning?"

"Good a place as any, I suppose."

"Do you know why he's here, in the Philippines?"

"No."

"Is that why you were following him, to find out?"

"Who said I was following him?"

"Mr. Belasko, don't try to obscure the obvious. I know what I know. And I know you were following him. I know you came here from Los Angeles, just like Mr. Harding. But, unlike you, I also know why he is here."

He kept calculating the odds on overpowering the young woman, but they never changed, and he didn't like them.

And he was getting interested, in spite of himself. "Go on," he said.

"How much do you know about my country?"

"Enough."

"You remember the Huks? Hukbalahap? You don't seem old enough."

"I know of them, yes."

"And the New People's Army? You know of them, too?"

"Yes."

"You know why they existed, the Huks, the NPA? Because of people like your Mr. Harding."

"Stop calling him that. He's not 'my' Mr. Harding. I don't know who the hell he belongs to, but it sure as hell isn't me."

"That's the American way, isn't it, Mr. Belasko? Let people be exploited, reap the rewards of that exploitation and disavow its architects. As long as you have two cars and three televisions, who cares about people who have to walk and who have no radio? 'Fuck 'em,'—isn't that the American attitude?"

"Lady, if there's an attitude around here, it's yours, and I'm sick of it. You don't know jackshit about me. Talk about black and white. If there's a blacker black and a whiter white than the colors you're seeing, I don't know where the hell they might be."

"Of course, I knew you'd get around to that, sooner or later. The oppressor always blames the oppressed. Resentment is the privilege of the overclass...."

The truck lurched suddenly, but she pushed on. "You always—"

"Stop it!" Bolan snapped suddenly.

"You—"

"I heard something. Be quiet!"

The truck was leaning perilously, and the growl of the engine gradually disappeared under an increasingly louder thumping, like that of approaching thunder.

"A flat tire," she said, "nothing to worry about. It happens a lot up here."

"No, before that. It was sharper. I heard it twice, no more than that."

"Maybe..."

The truck crashed into something, and Bolan was thrown forward, slamming into the front wall. The woman landed on top of him, and one elbow caught him in the temple. He saw a flash of bright light for a second, then felt the throbbing of his head.

"Are you hurt?" he asked.

She didn't answer him immediately, and he shook her by one shoulder as he squirmed out from under her. She must have been stunned for a few seconds. But as he extricated himself, he felt the cold, round mouth of the automatic press against the back of his neck.

"Don't move," she ordered.

He smelled gasoline and pounded on the front wall of the truck. "We have to get out of here," he said. He beat his fist on the wall, but no one responded. Then, off to his left, he saw the first orange flash. It flickered and vanished, like a serpent's tongue.

"Fire," he said. "We better get out of the truck. Now!"

"Don't try to fool me. I may be a woman, but I'm not stupid."

"Listen, we have to get out of the truck. It's starting to burn. If the fuel tank goes up, we won't have a chance in hell."

Something changed her mind, maybe the tone of his voice or perhaps she smelled the gasoline or the scorched vegetation wafting into the truck.

For the first time since he'd met her, she seemed genuinely frightened. Her voice broke when she said, "It's locked. From the outside."

9

Bolan reached for her hand. It trembled in his grasp, but she refused to let go of the pistol. "Let go, damn it!" he shouted. "Marisa, we have to get out of here."

"No!"

He twisted her arm, and the pistol clattered onto the floor of the truck. He groped for it in the dark, conscious of how little time they had left. The orange glow was already getting brighter. He found the pistol and crawled to the rear of the truck. He was too tall to stand upright, and knelt at the crack between the two doors.

Running his fingers along the joint between them, he found the bolts holding the latch in place. He fired two quick shots, with the muzzle held nearly flat against the sheet metal. Behind him Marisa screamed.

Lying on his back, he brought both feet back and slammed them into the door, one on either side of the latch. The doors bowed outward but did not give. He could feel the heat of the flames on his ankles as he pulled them back for another try.

Again he slammed both feet forward, ramming them like pile drivers into the door. This time one flew open. A wave of superheated air surged into the truck. "Marisa, come on," he shouted. In the dull orange glare, he turned to see her cowering in one corner of the truck.

He stuck the gun in his belt and scrambled toward her. She heard him coming, and shrank even farther into the corner. Without a word he grabbed her under the shoulders and hauled her to her feet. Bending at the waist, he pushed and shoved her toward the open door.

"Stay right there," he said, dropping to the ground. He reached back up for her, grabbed a knee in each hand and pulled. She toppled forward, and he caught her over his left shoulder. She was heavier than she looked, and the impact of her body nearly knocked him over.

He ran into the trees and set her down. "Wait here," he said.

"Don't leave me," she said. Her voice was emotionless, almost robotic, but he could sense the terror her inflection tried to conceal.

He sprinted back to the truck and yanked the driver's door open. The driver was slumped forward over the steering wheel. A gaping hole in his skull obscured the left temple. The bullet must have come from the opposite side of the road, Bolan thought as he pulled the driver free. The man was dead, and there was no time for courtesy. He let the body fall to the ground and reached for the second man in the cab. He, too, had been shot, through and through, also from the right side of the road. The glass of the windshield and the passenger window was a mass of cracks, glittering orange with reflected light.

As he backed out of the cab, Bolan snatched the passenger's M-16 and a canvas bag jammed down between the bucket seats. When he stepped down from the running board, he started to back away but tripped and fell. Scrambling to his feet, he noticed the flames now beginning to lick at the huge gas tank under the truck. He stumbled back into the trees, ignoring the slender branches slashing at his face and hands.

He found Marisa right where he'd left her, as if she had grown roots in the rich, loamy soil. He dropped to the ground beside her.

Bolan reached out to pat her knee. "I'm back," he said.

She said nothing, instead placing a finger to her lips. Thinking she must have heard something, Bolan cocked his head to one side, listening to the jungle. The only noise he could hear was the crackle of the flames.

"What is it," Bolan whispered, "what do you hear?"

As if in answer, the gas tank on the truck blew, sending a feathery plume of burning fuel high into the air. The trees between him and the truck looked black, as though they had been carved out of coal.

Marisa flinched at the thunderous explosion. "Juan?" she asked. "Pablito?"

"Dead," Bolan said. "I'm sorry."

Marisa shook her head. "No, you're not. Don't say it to spare my feelings. They were my friends, but you didn't know them."

Bolan marveled at the toughness that seemed as much a part of her as the flesh on her bones, the blood in her veins.

"What happened?" she asked.

"They didn't suffer, if that's what you want to know."

"Thank you for that, but, no, that's not what I want to know. I want to know what happened."

"Someone shot them both. From the right side of the road. An ambush."

"And you saw no one?"

"No."

"But they are still here, the ones who murdered Juan and Pablito. They are close by."

"How do you know?"

"I know because I just heard them. I know because it is always the same."

"Many?"

"Ten or twelve, probably. That is the way it usually goes."

"Then we have to get the hell out of here. Do you know where we are?"

"Yes."

"Then you have to guide me."

"We have to follow the road. That's the only way I know to guide you."

"We can't stay on the road. If there's a dozen men out there looking to kill us, we wouldn't stand a chance."

"We don't have far to go."

"How can you be sure?"

She laughed. "I may be frightened, Mr. Belasko, but I'm not stupid. I don't mean to walk in the middle of the road. But if you look closely, you'll realize there is only one road to choose from. Since I know where we were going, I know how to get there. I don't know how far, but it shouldn't be more than three or four miles. It's too bad we don't have Pablito's pack."

"You mean this?" Bolan placed the canvas bag in her lap.

She brushed it with her fingertips, then smiled a sad smile. "So, Pablito will help us get there yet. This is his bag."

She reached for the buckles holding the bag closed. One at a time, she undid the two straps, then slid her hand in under the canvas flap. When she withdrew her hand, she held a small transceiver. She brought the small black box to her lips and kissed it.

"You see?" she asked. "We can call the others and tell them to come get us."

"Then we'll have to stay here, near the truck. Otherwise they won't be able to find us."

"So...?"

"You know damn well what I'm talking about. You said yourself there is a dozen men out there. They're looking for us right now. We *can't* stay here."

"We have no choice."

"Maybe you don't, but I do," Bolan snapped.

"Fine, do whatever you want. At least leave me a gun."

"Don't do this, Marisa."

"Do what, Mr. Belasko?"

"Play on my sympathy."

"I'm surprised. You don't strike me as a man who would even have sympathy. For anyone. And if you think I am not above manipulating you, you're wrong. Do as you please. But I want to warn you that you can't get out of here without our help."

"I'll take my chances on that."

Marisa held up a hand. "Quiet," she ordered.

And this time Bolan heard it, too. Voices, too far away to be intelligible, but too close for comfort. It sounded as if the speakers were arguing.

"What are they saying?" Bolan whispered, bending close to bring his lips to Marisa's ear.

"They are trying to figure out how the driver got out of the truck."

She looked at him, her face asking him the same question.

"I had to move him," Bolan explained.

This time Marisa didn't bother to lean close, choosing instead to trust the air to keep her confidence. "They will be searching both sides of the road soon. You'd better hurry if you want to leave."

Bolan squeezed her hand. "No. And don't think it's charity. Listen, get on that radio. If they come too much closer, you won't be able to."

"What are you going to do?"

"That depends."

"On what?"

"On who they are. For all I know, they're the good guys."

"Trust me, Mr. Belasko, they're not. They are the Philippine equivalent of the Salvadoran death squads."

"Maybe, maybe not."

"Damn you, believe whatever you want...I don't care."

Bolan squeezed her hand again. "The radio..."

Then he was gone. "Be careful," she whispered after him.

Working his way silently through the trees, Bolan got as close to the ruined truck as he dared. It was still a raging inferno, the blackened metal hulk appearing and disappearing in the very center of an orange cauldron.

From his vantage point, he spotted seven or eight men standing in a ragged semicircle just beyond the reach of the flames. It would have been a sure thing to hit them. With any luck, he could take them all out with a single burst from the M-16. But until he knew what was what and who was who, he wasn't shooting anyone, especially not in the back.

The men were talking among themselves in Spanish. His command of the language was a bit rusty, but he understood enough to get the general drift of the conversation. One thing puzzled him, though. Marisa had said there would be ten to twelve men. That left as many as four unaccounted for.

As if in answer to his question, two more shadows suddenly appeared against the orange backdrop. As they approached the semicircle, the chattering men shut up. One of the two, then, must be their commanding officer.

"Speak English, damn it," one of the newcomers snapped.

"That's just like you Americans," the other said. "So fucking parochial. It's laughable that you should be one of the two most powerful countries in the world."

"Fuck you, Carbajal. When you want our help, you speak English pretty good. Don't go giving me any bullshit about being parochial. So I don't have any Spanish—big deal."

"So, where are the others, Mr. Johnson? If you know so much, tell me that."

"How the hell should I know? I already told you, they got wind of something. Everything's going to hell. The bastard the police talked to, Belasko, Belaski or whatever it was, must have known something. We almost nailed him in Manila, but he squeaked through. I'm telling you, he had to be in that truck. It's the only way he could have gotten out of Manila."

"Why is he so important?"

"If I knew that, I'd be a lot happier myself. All I know is, he was tailing Harding before the shit hit the fan at the airport. He was there when it went down. And now he runs down a fucking rabbit hole and disappears."

"And you think we should search the jungle in the middle of the night to find this man?"

"Yeah, I do. And I bet we find the broad with him," the American said.

"And if we do find him, then what?"

"Ice the fucker."

The other man sighed, then turned to the small group of men. In Spanish he ordered them to fan out from the truck and to shoot anything that moved.

That was all Bolan needed to know. Whatever the hell Marisa was up to, these guys were trouble. Plain and simple. He backed away from the burning truck, its light flickering through the shadows cast by tall trees around him.

Carefully he made his way toward the spot where he had left Marisa. Behind him he could hear the men beating the undergrowth. They were talking in loud voices to keep their fear at bay. He almost missed her as he moved past, not fifteen feet from where she lay coiled in a tight ball, trying to blend in with the floor of the forest or sink to the other side of the shadows.

Bolan moved back toward the hunters a few feet to interpose himself between Marisa and the searchers. Concealing himself among the fronds of a patch of tall ferns, he crouched down and waited.

He could see one of them moving straight toward him. The others had spread out to the left. Bolan steeled himself as the searcher drew closer. The fronds waved as the man pushed into them from the other side. Bolan waited until he took one more step. As he brushed by him, Bolan snaked an arm around his neck, crushing the windpipe and preventing him from shouting.

The man tried to breathe, and the gurgle in his throat dribbled away as Bolan exerted still more pressure, bracing his other forearm against the back of his captive's skull. With a sudden jerk, he snapped the neck. Easing up slightly, he felt the head loll to one side, then lowered the lifeless body gently to the ground.

It had been too damn near a miss. **And** Marisa was a liability, especially in the jungle. At all costs, they had to get closer to the road.

10

Bolan hauled Marisa up the slippery incline, his feet sliding on the damp, rotten leaves. The firing continued behind them, and stray slugs whined through the branches overhead, showering them both with tattered leaves. Just ahead the lip of the incline curved up nearly vertically. From fifty feet, it looked to be about five or six feet high, but it could be more. It was going to be close.

The nearest of their pursuers was no more than fifty yards behind them. Bolan kept tugging at Marisa's arm, until he thought it would pull out of its socket.

The dense jungle behind them swallowed nearly every sound except the gunfire. Bolan crossed mental fingers, hoping that Marisa's faith in her compatriots was not misplaced. If it were, it would be too late for her to regret it. Bolan tripped over a log, nearly buried in dark brown leaves. As he struggled to his feet, he lost his grip on the woman for a moment, and she cried out, afraid he had left her behind.

He clapped a hand, slippery with decayed vegetation, over her mouth and held it there until she stopped struggling. He leaned forward to whisper in her ear. "Come on, Marisa, hold it together. We're almost to the road. Okay?"

At first she didn't respond, but when he asked a second time, she nodded as best she could.

As he let go, he heard a rustle of leaves and dropped to the ground, pulling her down with him. Straining his eyes to see in the dark, he saw nothing that looked out of place. The rustling noise had stopped, but he was certain one of the search party was just behind a curtain of thick, umbrella-like leaves. A shot would alert the others, but he couldn't afford to turn his back on a threat that close.

"Wait here," he whispered. Bolan started to crawl toward the fan of broad leaves, spread open like the fingers of a huge hand. Keeping his eye fixed on the center of the fan, he moved one hand, then a leg, another hand, a second leg. He controlled his breath, taking deep gulps as seldom as he could and taking care to make no noise.

Since he had begun his approach, not a single leaf had fluttered. He was starting to think he had imagined the noise when he spotted something jutting out just past the face of a leaf. It could have been a twig or some sort of weird bug. Or the muzzle of an automatic rifle. Bolan squinted to sharpen the focus, but the effort was futile. There just wasn't enough light. Lying flat out, Bolan rolled onto his back, waited a few seconds, then rolled again to lie on his stomach about four feet to the left.

As he lay there, he listened for a long moment. The gunfire had tapered off a little, as if the men were trying to conserve ammunition. Or, Bolan though, maybe they had blown off their fear, and fired now only with some reasonable cause.

From his new vantage point, he could still see the projection. And now it looked just a little too perfect, a little too round. Back up on hands and knees, he crept farther to the left. Somehow he had to get in behind the thick leaves. He couldn't risk a head-on charge. Even if he didn't get himself killed, the noise of his assault would certainly draw the others.

Sharpening his angle away to the left, he climbed into a crouch, moving more quickly now. Fending off the thick undergrowth with his left arm, he slithered into a clump of feathery fronds and slipped up behind a thick-waisted tree trunk. The tree itself had snapped off a dozen feet from the ground, and it lay like a broken mast from some long-forgotten shipwreck.

Bolan crawled under the trunk and slid along behind it. Falling more and more deeply into a crouch as the tree's crown drew closer, he kept his eyes riveted on the motionless fronds. He was looking at them from the side now, but still saw nothing. As he reached the tangle of broken branches, he slid in among them, moving each one aside only far enough to get past it. Even the damp, rotten wood could give him away if one of the branches were to snap. He felt the slippery pulp of fungus under his fingertips, where molds of every kind slowly devoured the rotting branches.

As he bent the last branch and ducked under it, he found himself staring straight at the back of a man crouching in the shadows. Bolan cursed himself for not having the Beretta. Its sound suppressor made it perfect for use at the moment. But he didn't have it, and he was going to have to improvise.

The gunfire had dwindled away to occasional single shots. As the searchers spread out in the dense forest, the leaves muffled even those few, and they sounded as if they had come from a long way off.

Placing one foot on the thick carpet of moldering leaves, he leaned his weight forward, then tugged his other leg free of the branches. Holding the tip of his tongue between his teeth, he started forward, the M-16 ready. He closed to within five feet of the man when something snapped underfoot.

The man started to turn as Bolan took another step closer. Raising the assault rifle high in the air, like a pinch hitter trying to loosen up, he started his swing as the man's profile emerged from the shadows. Bolan saw the mouth open in surprise and the lips begin to form a word. As the rifle cracked against his temple, the man's mouth went slack. He sank straight down, as if a trap door had opened beneath him.

He lay there in a heap. Bolan bent over to feel for a pulse. There was one, but it was going to be a while before the crumpled form regained consciousness. Quickly Bolan disentangled the unconscious man's arm from the leather sling of his AK-47, slung it over his own shoulder, then knelt to see what else of use he could find.

The man wore a Browning 9 mm automatic in a canvas holster hooked on a garrison belt. Bolan undid the belt, tugged it loose and rebuckled it, then draped it over the same shoulder as the AK. Three ammo pouches, one small, probably for the Browning, and two larger, for the AK-47, dangled from the belt, along with a pair of M-59 grenades.

Bolan pushed through the thick, rubbery leaves and sprinted back toward Marisa. She stood where he had left her. Her head was cocked to one side, and she turned slightly as he approached, as if to hear him better. He reached for her outstretched hand and continued on past, barely slowing his pace. She spun in her tracks and fell in behind him, doing her best to match his stride.

As the slope grew steeper, she got the better of him. His weight kept him sliding on the slimy mulch while she seemed to skate on it with effortless grace. When they reached the final ascent, he had to pause for a moment. They were flush up against a vertical wall. It was a good foot taller than Bolan.

"I'll have to lift you up," he whispered. "Just raise your hands over your head and get a solid grip on something."

He pressed his back against the wall of vegetation and tugged Marisa toward him. "Okay," he said, "give me your foot."

He made a stirrup of his hands and slipped it under the sole of Marisa's boot. She bounced once, twice, and on the third time, he lifted as she sprang upward. Her hands thrashed in the growth on top of the wall, and suddenly her weight started to decrease. He realized she'd found a hand-hold and begun to pull herself up. He pulled upward on his linked hands, and she slid up and over him. A moment later she was gone.

Bolan kicked holes in the embankment with the toes of his boots, driving them through the mushy greenery and into the sticky clay behind it. With the second toehold secure, he could reach up and far over the edge to find a sturdy bush rooted deeply enough to bear his weight.

As he pulled himself up and over, he heard the unmistakable sound of an approaching engine. It was just a notch above idle, as if the driver were coasting along, using his engine only enough to keep from rolling to a stop. Bolan got to his knees, only now aware that the jungle had fallen silent behind him. The firing had stopped, and nothing else moved among the trees. The monkeys and the birds seemed to be waiting for something else to happen. Even the tree frogs were silent.

They still had twenty yards to cover before they reached the road itself. Bolan hauled Marisa to her feet and plunged down into the thick undergrowth. He was less concerned about the noise now.

He had to admire Marisa and her people, at least for their efficiency if nothing else. The jeep was right on time. He didn't want to think about what might happen if he was wrong, if it wasn't the jeep they were waiting for. It just had to be, and that's how they were playing it.

They broke into the open so suddenly that Bolan hadn't seen it coming. In knee-high grass, he stumbled to a halt. A hundred yards away, little more than a block of shadow on wheels, a jeep rolled toward them, its lights out. Bolan fell flat in the tall grass and tugged Marisa down beside him.

"Okay," he said into her ear, "there's a jeep just up the road. See if you can raise him on the radio."

Marisa tugged the small transceiver from a deep pocket in her jacket. So softly that Bolan wasn't even sure she had spoken, she repeated the same phrase twice. It was in a language completely alien to him. He guessed it must be Tagalog. In answer, the jeep flashed its headlights once.

"That's Carlos," she whispered.

They heard scrambling behind them, at the bottom of the wall, and Bolan decided they'd better not wait. "Come on," he said, getting to his feet.

Marisa got up without help this time. She groped in the air for his hand. When she found it, she curled her fingers around his and squeezed a moment, then let go. He nodded to himself, and started down the gentle slope to the road. The jeep was still idling its way along, and Bolan stepped into the hard-packed dirt of the road about twenty yards in front of it. He could see the silhouettes of two men in the front seat.

He stuck out an arm to brake Marisa to a halt, and they waited impatiently for the jeep to cover the last fifty feet. The driver braked and rolled to a stop right beside Bolan.

"Get in quickly," he said in an urgent, low tone.

Bolan boosted Marisa into the jeep and climbed into the back seat alongside of her. Kicking the trans into reverse, the driver backed into a tight K, and dropped into first. The gears whined and Bolan heard shouting from the thick brush.

"Step on it," he barked.

The driver floored it, and the jeep spurted forward, its tires slipping momentarily on the damp clay surface of the road. The driver shifted into second, and the engine roared until he popped the clutch. A burst of rifle fire spanged into the ass end of the jeep and whined off into the jungle on the far side of the road.

They rounded a curve just as another burst, this time from several weapons, raked the clay all around them. A moment later they were out of sight. The gunmen continued to fire, spraying the jungle in the vain hope that a lucky slug might take out a tire. Over the roaring of their engine, the gunfire faded away. Rounding a second curve, the driver clicked on his headlights and shifted into third.

The road wound ahead of them, twisting and turning, as if it were trying to evade the blinding glare of the headlights. The driver was good, but the slippery road made it tough to control the jeep on the tighter curves. Even the thick treads of the jeep's tires struggled to hang on. The careering vehicle yawed wildly before the tires bit, then it lurched ahead, gaining speed until the driver braked into a skid at the next curve, fought to regain control, only to repeat the process in succession again.

"What's that up ahead?" Bolan shouted, tapping the driver on the shoulder.

The driver shouted something Bolan couldn't catch over the screaming engine. Two pairs of orange rectangles seemed to hover in the air about a quarter mile ahead. They were in a long straightaway, and the jeep was picking up speed.

Closing fast on the hovering lights, they were only a hundred yards away when Bolan realized it was a pair of jeeps, their parking lights lit, straddling the roadway.

A sudden explosion, like a meteor shower, lanced overhead. Bolan recognized the hammering of an M-60 immediately. The driver spun the wheel sharply, and the jeep skidded several feet broadside before its tires bit, then it plunged into the tall grass alongside the road. The M-60 stabbed at them again, tracers ripping the darkness as they homed in. Carlos had killed his lights and was barreling straight ahead. The jeep canted to one side as it rocked over the uneven ground beneath the grass.

Bolan swung his M-16 up and sprayed an entire clip, aiming just above the hoods of the two jeeps. He was rewarded by a cascade of shattering glass. The M-60 stopped instantly, and they plunged on past. Bolan jammed a second clip into the M-16 and cut loose again.

This time the others in the blockade fired back. Their rifles ripped at the careering jeep in search of flesh. Bolan pulled the pin on one of his two grenades and tossed it backward. The deadly hook shot found the rim and dropped in between the two pairs of orange lights. It went off almost at once. In the sudden fireball, he could see one jeep upend while the other rocked over on two wheels, then settled back just as its gas tank blew.

An orange cloud mushroomed up into the night.

They were safe for the moment.

11

Bolan sat in the jeep, taking it all in. The camp was a model of efficiency. More than a dozen buildings, and not a single one could be seen from the air, so cleverly had they been woven in and around the rain forest. Even the clearing at its heart looked pristine.

It was beginning to brighten, and Bolan glanced at his watch. It was five-thirty, and the sun was due in just a few minutes. In another hour or two, the morning mist would burn off, and by midday, everyone alive in this part of Luzon would be counting the minutes until sundown. Bolan had seen similar places before, though none so economically designed. It was the precision that stunned him, and bothered him more than a little. Just this cursory examination convinced him that Marisa's group was not just a spontaneous movement of inexperienced peasants.

The camp had something of the textbook about it, something of the ideal that is seldom approached in field conditions. And never achieved.

And yet, here it was. Picture perfect.

Why? The question rattled around Bolan's brain like a runaway pinball. Who the hell were these people? And what did they *really* want? The most troublesome question was who was helping them to get it?

Marisa had promised that answers to his questions would be forthcoming. He doubted that more than most things, and Mack Bolan was a man who took very little on faith. As

he sat there, the sky turned a milky white. The sun must
have risen above the mountains now, but the morning soup
was still too thick for its color to come through.

The others had left him unattended, as though he posed
no threat to them. They were either supremely confident of
their position, or Marisa had been telling him the truth.
Neither seemed too likely, and yet, there he was, alone in the
middle of the Luzon jungle, in the very heart of the guer-
rilla camp, and no one seemed to give a damn.

He climbed down from the jeep to stretch his legs,
reached over the bullet-scarred rear panel and snatched the
canvas bag Marisa had left behind. With nothing better to
do, he decided to go through it. Bolan dropped the bag on
the hood and unbuckled the flaps. And there were his Beretta 93-R and his .44 AutoMag, each wrapped carefully in
oiled cloth. It seemed that Marisa and her people even worried about rust.

Somewhere behind the semicircle of thatched huts, a
rooster cut loose. Almost as if it had been a signal, Marisa
reappeared in the doorway through which she had gone five
minutes before. Behind her a tall man, a thatch of unruly
red hair tumbling over sun-leathered skin, ducked under the
lintel and followed her.

Bolan studied the man as he approached. About six three
or four, he looked to weigh no more than a hundred and
ninety, if that. He had an easy gait, a casual, almost jaunty
walk that was as far from Charles Harding's ramrod strut
as it could be. His shoulders were broad, and even under the
camou shirt, Bolan could see the power of the man.

The tall man draped an arm over Marisa's shoulder,
guiding her gently with pressure from his fingers. When they
were three feet away, he let the arm fall and Marisa stopped.
She held out a hand, and Bolan took it in his own. Then,
turning slightly and moving a step away, she allowed the tall
man to take her place. He, too, held out a hand as Marisa
said, "Mr. Belasko, this is Tom Colgan."

Bolan tried not to react. Marisa, of course, couldn't see him. Colgan himself, though, was another matter. Bolan could hear Frank Henson's voice in his head, saying "Colgan" over and over again. He noticed the man's eyes and wondered just how much they could see. Like two blue beacons, they burned with a dark light, set deep in the leathery skin. Bolan had the funny feeling that Colgan could look right through him, even see the bones buried deep inside him, as if looking at an X ray. The eyes looked as though they had a life of their own. He'd seen eyes like them before, but not lately. They were the eyes of a madman or, perhaps worse, a zealot.

The tall man clasped Bolan's hand in both of his own and shook it warmly. "Tom is my husband," Marisa said.

"I see," Bolan replied.

She laughed. "I don't think you do." The laughter was genuine, as if some great pressure inside her had been mysteriously released or a weight lifted from her shoulders by an unseen hand.

"I've been waiting to meet you, Mr. Belasko. You are wondering how I knew you were coming. I understand. Let's get you something to eat. We can talk over breakfast."

Bolan nodded. "Fine."

"This way," Colgan said. He turned, and without waiting to see whether Bolan would follow, he walked toward one end of the half moon of buildings. Marisa followed, glancing back at Bolan over her shoulder.

Bolan fell in behind the couple, wondering what other surprises lay in store for him. That there would be more was beyond question. Colgan ducked to enter the last building on the left, and Marisa disappeared right after him. Bolan hesitated for a moment, then stepped into the dimly lit interior.

The mess hall was functionally laid out; four rows of tables and benches, all roughly hewn from the same raw wood, ran the length of the building, leaving aisles after every pair to make navigation easier. A door, similar to the one he'd just entered, sat in the middle of the far wall, and two more opposed one another at either end.

One of the tables was already set for three. The simple tin dishes and Army-issue utensils brought Bolan back years to a time he'd rather forget. Colgan helped Marisa slide in between bench and table, then sat across from her. He nodded toward the remaining plate, next to Marisa, and said, "Help yourself. We don't stand on ceremony here."

Bolan looked at the food, mostly rice with an admixture of a stringy red vegetable—somewhere between pimiento and pepper—and thick hunks of something that was probably fish.

Bolan took a mouthful, tasted it cautiously, then swallowed. It wasn't bad, but it was not going to be the latest rage in nouvelle cuisine, either.

While they ate, Colgan began to fill him in. "Marisa tells me you don't know very much about Charles Harding."

"That's right," Bolan said.

"But you were following him." Bolan noticed that it was a statement, not a question. "Look, you don't have to say anything. I know what I know. And I know you were following him. What I know, and you don't, is why."

"Oh?" Bolan raised an eyebrow at that.

"That think-tank charade is pure fluff, garbage, window dressing, for Christ's sake. That nonsense is about as legitimate as three-card monte on a New York street corner."

"Then what is he really up to?"

"I only know part of it," Colgan said, reaching for a tin cup to wash some of the rice down with tepid water. "Look, Belasko, let's be honest with one another. Harding is fronting, maybe even masterminding, although I can't prove it, a plot to overthrow the Aquino government. That's why he is here, and that's what he's been doing ever since she took over."

"And I suppose you're a white knight who plans to rescue the lady from the dragon."

"Something like that, yes. But the lady is not who you think she is, Mr. Belasko. The lady is not Corazon Aquino—she is the Republic of the Philippines."

"So you tried to have Harding iced...." Bolan watched Colgan chew one of the chunks of fish, reach in gingerly to pull a small white bone from between his teeth and shake his head in disagreement.

"No," he argued. "That business at the airport was his people."

Bolan grunted. "What'd he do, make off with the treasury?"

"Nope. It's probably a lot simpler than that."

"Oh, really?"

"Yes, really."

"Then why?"

"Because you were following him. Maybe they were after you, Mr. Belasko. Maybe it's even as simple as that. The people behind him are scared. They're a special breed. I call them the mushrooms. They only grow in the dark, and the more shit around them, the better they like it."

"And you think that's why I was following him? To let some light into the cellar?" Bolan scooped a forkful of the sticky rice into his mouth. It was getting cold, and the grains were clumping together into a pasty mass in his mouth. He dropped the fork and let it lie on the table. "Well, I'll tell you something, Mr. Colgan. You couldn't be further off the mark."

"Whatever you say."

"If you know something, Colgan, spit it out. Otherwise let's just shut up and eat whatever the hell this is. And I'll be on my way."

"Look, you think things are okay here. You think, now that Marcos is gone, the Philippines can settle down to a nice, quiet Third World siesta. Mama Aquino is here to spank people like me who get out of line, so Uncle Sam can sleep well at night. But it isn't like that. You know, most Americans think reality is what's in the newspapers. But they're dead wrong. Reality is what people don't let into the papers. It's Ollie North and Rose Mary Woods, Lee Harvey Oswald and Gavrilo Princip. It's what's in the fucking *dark*, Belasko, that's what reality is.''

"So where does Harding come in?"

"That's what I'm trying to tell you, man. Harding is just one of them. And not the most significant. In this chess game, he's a bishop, no more. But the queen, Belasko, the *queen*, that's where the power lies. And she's down there somewhere, in the dark, planning it all, trying to reshape the Philippines in the image of Ferdinand Marcos. He was the liaison man, the conduit between the Pentagon and the Leyte Brigade.''

"Never heard of it," Bolan said, not particularly impressed.

"You will, and you can take that to the bank. Unless..."

"Unless what?"

"Unless we manage to uproot it, kill it, let it lie there in the bright sun and shrivel up like a dandelion. These are fucking vampires Belasko, that's what we're talking about. They need the darkness, deep cover. They know every trick in the book, everything from false flags to bamboo under the fingernails. They have money and they have connections, in Aquino's government and in the Pentagon. That's what it's all about. Getting rid of Aquino and replacing her with a right-wing government. Generals in her own army get drunk and talk about setting her head out on a stake. This is not kindergarten here, man. And you have been sent to school without your textbooks. You better be a quick learner, Mr. Belasko.''

"Then why doesn't anyone know about it in the States?"

"They do, damn it, they do. But only a few people, people with one hand in the cash drawer and the other wrapped around a gun butt."

"Who, then. The CIA?"

"That's the bogey man, Belasko, kid stuff to scare liberals around their campfires. No, nothing that simple...."

"Who, then? The NSA...?"

"I'm not sure."

Bolan laughed outright. "You expect me to buy your joke and you don't even have a punchline. That's just plain pathetic, Colgan."

"Oh, you think so, do you?"

"Yeah, I do."

"Then answer me one simple question."

"Shoot."

"Why *were* you following Harding?" Bolan stared at him. Colgan had a hook, and Bolan could see him debating whether or not to twist it a little deeper into his flesh. But the look faded, and Colgan smiled instead. "Forget I said that."

"No, you're right. But something tells me you *do* know." He locked his eyes on Colgan's. Neither man blinked.

"All right, fair enough." Colgan smiled more broadly. "Something tells me we're on the same side, whether you know it or not. I'll tell you what I know, which isn't much. Two months ago, on Harding's last trip back here, somebody else was following him. We knew about him, just like we knew about you." He held up a cautionary finger. "Don't ask, because I can't tell you how. Anyway, we lost track of Harding and the tail. The next thing we knew, Harding was back in the States. The other guy finally turned up in a sewer in Ongpin."

"That could be a coincidence," Bolan suggested.

"I'll grant you that," Colgan replied. "It *could* be."

"But you don't think so...."

"No. Mr. Belasko, I don't."

"Do you want to tell me why?"

Colgan nodded. "Sure. Because that was the third time it happened. Three tails, and three corpses. The odds against that sort of thing are rather high, if not astronomical."

"I gather you have someone pretty high up in D.C., somebody in a position to feed you information."

"Naturally. But our source can't get a fix on Harding from that end, and we never managed to pull it off on this end, either."

"Tell me something," Bolan said. "If Harding always managed to get away from his tail, and the corpse showed up days later, with no fanfare, why would his own people try to take me out in such a public way? Why call attention to themselves? It doesn't make sense."

"That's true, and I don't have an explanation for it. Or, rather, I should say I don't have anything but conjecture."

"And that is?"

"You, Mr. Belasko. It has something to do with you. If the situation is not different, then the tail *must* be. It's just simple logic, after all."

Bolan shook his head but said nothing.

Colgan did not amplify, and Bolan finally stood up.

"Marisa will show you to your quarters. Get cleaned up. I'll see you in an hour or so," Colgan said. "I know you don't believe me. But after you see what I have to show you, you will. I think you'll want to join the team. And we have a lot to do. The mushrooms are waiting, Mr. Belasko. They're waiting for *us*."

"THAT'S TWICE you let him slip through your fingers." Charles Harding leaned back in his chair, folding his hands behind his head. "I'm beginning to wonder if you can cut it anymore."

The man across from him said nothing. There was nothing he could say, and he knew it.

"Cordero is doing his part. We're so close I can almost smell the cordite. I don't want any more screwups. Do you understand?"

The man nodded. "I still don't see what the big deal is about this guy."

"No, I don't suppose you do. But then, I'm not surprised. You let some two-bit sawbones with a messiah complex run you like a damn rabbit. How the hell can I expect you to understand what this man is?"

"Maybe if you weren't so damn secretive..."

Harding tilted forward. The legs of his chair slammed into the wooden floor. "The man is not one of those ordinary baboons they've been sending—that's the first thing you have to get through that dense skull of yours. He's different. You know what happened at the airport. For crying out loud, man, you were *there*. You saw what he did. You think that's an ordinary jerk from some desk at the State Department?"

"No, of course not."

"Well then? What in the hell *do* you think?"

"I think it'd be a lot easier taking him out if you gave us more information."

"I don't have anything more than I gave you. I'm working on it, but every well I drill is dry. That ought to tell you something. It sure tells me something. This guy is poison. Somebody knows we've got a pipeline, and they flushed this guy down the chute to smoke us out. He doesn't have to nail me to be useful to them, and that's the whole point. Whatever happens to him—and I don't think they worry a hell of a lot about it—they learn something. Something they don't know now. Get it?"

"I guess so..."

Harding exploded. "Damn it, man, there is no room for guessing. Not now, not this late. The clock is ticking, and we can't stop it. Too much has been set in motion. I can't call Cordero off now."

"We'll get him, don't you worry."

"I *do* worry. That's why I'm here and you're on that side of the desk. You don't have brains enough to worry. You don't realize this man could bring us down."

"I'm telling you, he won't. I'll take care of it. Whatever it takes, it'll get done. You can bank on that."

"Banks fail. I don't believe in banks. I believe in graveyards and tombstones. That's what granite is for. That's what carved in stone means. Finished. Final. I want a tombstone over that son of a bitch. And I want it now!"

12

"It's not far," Colgan said, climbing into the front seat and nodding to the driver.

"What is it you want to show me?" Bolan asked.

"You know what they say about the picture and the thousand words?" Bolan acknowledged he knew the cliché, and Colgan went on. "Well, if that's what a picture's worth, I'd need a thousand pictures. It's easier if you just see for yourself."

The driver sensed that the conversation had ended for the moment, and kicked the clutch. The jeep jolted, then the gears engaged and it settled into a steady roll.

The sun had burned through the mist, and Bolan was stunned by the beauty of the valley. Far to the east, the rugged Sierra Madre range looked like a silver ripsaw standing on the top edge of its blade. Beyond it, Bolan knew, the Pacific stretched for thousands of miles, its rolling swells barely disturbed by the occasional island.

To the west, the even more majestic Cordillera Central ran through the middle of the Luzon, as hard and unyielding as a spine in the back of a trout. In the lowlands the jungle was bigger than a universe. Mile after mile of green, broken by spectacular sprays of red and yellow, blue and orange, and a purple so brilliant it seared the retina. Everything in the forest seemed to move in a hurry. Birds and butterflies, each trying to outdo the other with the extravagance of its colors, milled among the thick green leaves, flashing past and vanishing in an instant.

It was on this very island that a generation of young men, now slow, gray grandfathers, had fought the Japanese. It was on this same island that a younger generation of Filipinos fought against the remnants of colonial oppression with the passion and naiveté so typical of young men. The first generation had won and the second had lost. And of the survivors, very few of either generation knew for certain what had been gained and how much it had cost.

That history was all around. Helmets rusted on the jungle floor, little more useful than the broken shells of coconuts. Ruined rifles lay buried in leaves, their wooden stocks long since crumbled away. The tangled growth even swallowed the ruins of Mustangs and Zeros, hardly more now than rusting skeletons.

Bolan stared into the trees as if looking for ghosts. If he looked hard enough and long enough, he knew they'd be there. Glancing at Colgan, he tried to read the man's mind, but the body language was confusing, contradictory. On the one hand, he looked as relaxed and confident as any man Bolan had ever seen. He seemed to be perfectly at home in his surroundings. But deep inside Colgan something was ticking away, second by second, some unknown number was approaching zero. Bolan didn't want to think what might happen then.

"Hang on," the driver said, derailing Bolan's train of thought. He spun the wheel and nudged the jeep into a narrow lane. The trees grew so close to either side of the passage that Bolan could have spread his arms and touched one with the fingers of each hand. The grass was yellowed in twin stripes, the ground beneath it rutted, showing frequent, though not recent, passage.

Colgan turned to him, moved his lips twice, then shook his head. He had wanted to say something, but couldn't find the words. Finally he settled for a pointing finger. "Up ahead, not far."

The trees began to recede from the lane. Their branches still interlaced overhead, but the driver was able to relax a little with the added leeway. The lane widened farther, then vanished altogether as they broke into a wide, grassy meadow. Twin tracks of grassless clay ran straight as an arrow across the open field. The driver shifted down as the land began to climb at a steeper angle.

Colgan started to fidget. His shoulders kept squirming, and his head swiveled from side to side. Over Colgan's shoulder, Bolan could see one knee jumping as Colgan tapped his foot restlessly on the floor of the jeep. They reached the top of the rise, and the jeep tilted forward as they began a shallow descent.

A rank of trees marched toward them, the advance guard of an army. Bugs swarmed in the air and buzzed angrily around their heads. Bolan slapped at something that stung his neck and brought his hand away with the pulped insect still quivering in his palm. He looked at it with distaste, then scraped it off on the back wall and rubbed his palm clean on his pants.

This stand of trees was thinner, and Bolan could see the bright sparkle of reflected light among them. The water rippled, sending slashes of white through the leaves. The jeep entered the trees again, and the driver eased off on the accelerator.

Colgan tapped the driver on the shoulder. "Okay, Carlos. We'll walk now. You wait here."

Carlos killed the engine, and the jeep rolled to a halt. Colgan sat for a minute, as if holding an internal debate, then climbed down. Bolan followed him, shifting the M-16 from his lap to his shoulder in the same motion.

Colgan headed downhill, toward the water. Bolan fell in beside him. "You ready to tell me what this is all about?" he asked.

Colgan shook his head. "I already told you—you'll see for yourself."

They were fifty yards from the water when they broke out of the trees. Close up, Bolan saw the sparkle for the lie it was. The water, like all tropical rivers, was greenish brown. It moved sluggishly. No more than two hundred feet wide, it swept past them in a broad, shallow arc. On the far shore a flight of wading birds took off with frightened squawks, their wings beating air and water, then just air as they lifted off, trailing their long, snakelike legs behind them.

Monkeys in the forest on the far side shrilled, frightening parrots, which erupted like colored clouds and disappeared. An abrupt silence descended on them. When Colgan spoke, he whispered. "This way," he said. He headed upriver. On the uneven slope, his stride was stiff and awkward, that of a man whose legs no longer bent the way they should.

Looking ahead, Bolan saw several charred black squares. He knew immediately what they were. A village had been razed, the huts burned to nothing. The stumps of their stilts stuck up like black thumbs. Heaps of ashes marked the contours of the village. He had seen it a thousand times in Vietnam. It was almost humbling, how quickly a home could turn to dust. A year from now, there would be no trace of this place. Already plants had rooted in the ash. Thick clumps of greenish-silver grass had sprouted, pushing the ashes up into small cones like volcanoes spewing green lava.

Over the entire scene, something ominous and oppressive choked Bolan, constricting his throat. He could smell it, and he knew what it was. But Colgan pushed on, seemingly oblivious. And Bolan followed.

Carefully Colgan avoided stepping on the first patch of ashes, drifting toward the waterline before advancing again. There was something ceremonial in the action. It was the act of a man visiting a sacred shrine. Colgan's head was slumped forward on his chest, almost as if he were praying.

Methodically he threaded his way among the rectangular smears. Each of them bled downward, where rain had washed some of the ash toward the river.

The smell got stronger. Against the tree line, on the far side of the ruined village, a long, low mound ran perpendicular to the river. It was already half-green, covered with snaking vines, and grass sprouted haphazardly. Even flowers had taken root in the overturned earth.

Colgan stepped ten feet from the mound. The smell was overpowering now, and both men pinched their noses to keep it at bay. "There," Colgan muttered, his voice strangely unaffected. "There it is. Seventy-three men, women and children. Practically the entire population of the village that used to stand right here."

He turned his head slowly, in a dreamlike silence, to see if Bolan understood what he was being told.

Bolan nodded his head. "What happened?" he asked.

"The Leyte Brigade. That's what happened. Charles Harding's handiwork, if you will."

"How do you know?"

"I know, that's all. Never mind how."

Colgan dropped to one knee and crossed himself. Bolan watched quietly as Colgan's lips ran through a silent prayer. When he had finished, Colgan stood up. He started to back away from the mound, then snapped his head sharply and turned away. Bolan noticed the tears, but said nothing.

Head down, Colgan picked his way back through the ashes. He walked down toward the water and sat on a patch of grass. Bolan followed and took a seat next to him.

"Want to tell me about it?" he asked.

Colgan nodded his head. He opened his mouth, gasping like a landed trout, then swallowed hard. "Marisa was here when it happened. Her grandmother is buried back there." Colgan pointed toward the mound without turning to look.

"And you're certain Harding had something to do with this?"

"Not personally, at least as far as I can prove, but his organization, yes. Without a doubt. Marisa was here. She saw it all. Do you understand? She *saw* it happen. They shot her in the head, left her for dead. She survived, but..."

Bolan didn't know what to say. He stared at the water, watching the play of light on its sluggish surface.

Colgan sighed. "You know, I can't understand why it always has to be this way. I just can't understand it."

"It doesn't," Bolan said.

Colgan turned to look at him. "You think that Marcos was the problem here. You think since he's gone, it doesn't have to be this way, but you're dead wrong. Marcos was only part of the problem. Now Aquino is the problem. Not because she's corrupt like Marcos, but because the same corruption is still there. The body rots from the inside out. You don't cure cancer by changing skins. That's cosmetics, not medicine. And it sure as hell isn't a cure. Aquino is a puppet and doesn't know it. She'll learn, but not before it's too late. It's too late already."

Colgan stood and turned his back to Bolan. Staring out at the wriggling surface of the dark water, he knotted his fists, squeezing his fingers into his palms as if he wanted to kill a tiny insect in each hand.

"The mushrooms, Belasko. Do you understand?" He whirled suddenly, waving a wild hand in a broad arc toward the mounds of ashes. Then, one long trembling finger extended, he pointed to the burial mound. "The stink of that will never leave me. Not as long as Charles Harding, and men like him, are free to walk the earth like decent human beings."

Bolan watched Colgan's face. Veins bulged at his temples, and his eyes seemed to pulse blue light as they bored into the big guy.

"Do you know what it's like to be me, Belasko? I take human life, and I'm a doctor, for Christ's sake. A doctor... and I would throttle that man until his head snapped off like a dead flower. Me. A doctor..." He turned away again.

But the trembling finger still pointed its accusation, as if calling a jury's attention to a crucial fact it had overlooked.

But there was only Bolan to see, hear, and come to a conclusion.

13

Carlos was leaning against the jeep as Bolan made his way uphill. Colgan had wanted to stay behind for a moment, and Bolan understood. At the jeep he tried to engage Carlos in conversation, but the young man was anything but talkative. He gave polite, distant one-word answers, and after three tries, it was time to give up.

The sun beat down unmercifully, and Bolan wiped the sweat from his neck and forehead with a shirtsleeve. The insects seemed to be drawn to him, and hovered in small black clouds. They buzzed distantly, swarmed in like Stukas, the buzz growing louder and louder, then veered off as he swatted at them, the noise fading again to a distant hum.

He kept thinking about what Marisa and Colgan had told him. The idea that a quasi-sanctioned American operation had been actively attempting to undermine the Aquino government would have seemed farfetched a few years ago. But the world had changed, and the rule of law was getting more than a little frayed around the edges.

Frustration appeared to make lawbreakers out of the best of men. Maybe it was to be expected. Maybe it was even acceptable, but he didn't think so. A great deal could go wrong. The world was far too complicated to allow loose cannons to roll around. Somebody had to be in charge, and according to the Constitution, that man was the President. Until further notice, anyway. The trouble was, too many people close to the President thought he ought to have more power than the Constitution gave him. So they did whatever they could to get him the result they knew he wanted. And to protect him, they lied about it. They lied to the President himself, to Congress, to the people, and most of them, Bolan knew, also lied to themselves.

But even if he took Colgan's words at face value, there were many unknowns. Who the hell was the man, anyway? Not New People's Army, clearly. And why would a right-wing paramilitary organization, with U.S. funding and connivance of high-ranking Philippine Army officers, give a damn about him?

There was more to things than Colgan had told him—that was for certain. And where did the man's money come from? As Bolan mulled over the dozen mysteries, he watched Colgan climb the hill toward him, winding among the trees to appear for a moment, then vanish, only to appear again ten yards closer.

Colgan broke into the open and kicked at the grass as he climbed slowly toward the jeep. He heaved himself in and sat with his hands in his lap, staring at his feet. Bolan climbed over the back of the jeep and sat behind him. Carlos seemed unaware of anything as he finished puffing on his cigarette, letting the smoke out in long, thin streams through his nostrils. He fieldstripped the butt after a last, short drag, then got behind the wheel.

Carlos started the engine, took a sidelong glance at Colgan, then threw it in gear. They bounced through the ruts and up over the ridge. Carlos let the jeep coast down toward the trees, then dropped a gear to navigate the narrow mouth of the lane leading back to the road.

"What exactly are you and what are you trying to do here, Mr. Colgan?" Bolan asked.

"I'm trying to be a rational alternative to violence, Mr. Belasko. That's what I am and what I believe, with every fiber of my being, is the only way for the Filipino people to drag themselves out of the poverty and the desolation that has held them down for three hundred years."

Bolan grunted. "Rather idealistic, don't you think?"

"Maybe. But I can't do it any other way. I came here for the first time twenty-five years ago, with the Peace Corps. I'll never forget it as long as I live. I went home at the end of my tour, and I thought I'd be happy if I never saw another case of leprosy, or another malnourished baby, for the rest of my life. But I was wrong. It haunted me, Belasko, it ate at me day and night. I knew about the NPA, and I knew that wasn't the way. Too many people have given their hearts and souls to grass-roots movements only to be betrayed by their leaders. It happened in Cuba, it happened in Nicaragua, in Ethiopia, in Angola. I knew it could happen here and I thought perhaps I could do something about it."

"And have you?"

"I think so. I'm proud of what we've accomplished in only five years."

"What have you accomplished?"

"We've built a dozen clinics for free medical care, not just on Luzon, but throughout the archipelago. More than fifty people have been put through school, and now they are working with us as lawyers, engineers and so on. We even have eleven doctors we have trained."

"And you think that can make a difference?"

"I know it can."

"In my experience, the only way to beat an extremist is to play by his rules. You have to be willing to do anything he's willing to do. Because if you're not, sooner or later he'll discover that fact, and the minute he does, he's won. He might as well have nuclear weapons. After all," Bolan said, shaking his head, "there has never been a moderate revolution."

"That's where you're wrong, Mr. Belasko. There was one."

"Oh, really?"

"The American revolution. There's never been anything like it. And I think it's high time we started teaching the rest of the world there is another way. Your philosophy only perpetrates the bloodshed, extends the killing through another generation. You don't teach people anything by shooting them, but you teach their children something."

"Then why do you have guns?"

"Because no matter what, I am still a realist."

He turned and watched the trees go by. Colgan seemed preoccupied as the jeep broke back into the open. Bolan studied him carefully. There was something of the charlatan about the man, and something of the zealot. It almost seemed as if he weren't really in the same world. That Colgan had been genuinely moved by the visit was clear. But little else about him came even close to being transparent.

The sulking-hermit routine seemed to Bolan almost too pat, as if it had been carefully rehearsed until every second had been plotted with the exactness of science. It looked fine, until you looked closely. It was like a cheap tinfoil bell on a Christmas tree—with the right lighting, it could be a crown jewel, but in the harsh light of day, one couldn't conceal just how tawdry it really was.

He wanted to push Colgan, but now wasn't the time. So soon after the theatrics, it would give the man an excuse to retreat behind wounded feelings. That he would be a marvel in that role was a certainty. Timing was everything, not only for Colgan, but for Bolan himself. And his gut told him something was askew. Only two possibilities suggested themselves. If Colgan was what he tried so hard to seem, then the man was mad. And if he was anything else, then he was, at the very least, a fraud. Neither choice boded well.

With Henson wasted, Bolan was up a very tall tree, way out on a limb without a telephone or a parachute. And he didn't have to close his eyes to imagine Colgan himself laughing over the snarl of a chainsaw. And yet he couldn't shake the feeling that Marisa was as genuine as Colgan seemed not to be. How could she not see what Bolan saw? How could she live with this man, watch him manipulate others so easily and not understand that he was using everyone he touched?

Up ahead Bolan spotted a second jeep, sitting just off the narrow road among the trees. He tapped Carlos on the shoulder and pointed. The kid nodded, then pointed the jeep out to Colgan. They started to slow down as Carlos stepped on the clutch and coasted a bit before shifting down a gear.

Colgan waved his arms over his head, and someone in the other jeep responded with the same gesture. Carlos nosed his jeep to the left and let it roll through the tall grass. Branches raked at his side of the jeep and snapped under the heavy tires. Bolan recognized neither of the two men in the other vehicle.

Carlos let his jeep roll to a stop, almost bumper to bumper with the other. Colgan climbed down and waved to Bolan to follow him. The driver of the other jeep dangled one leg over the side and turned to take Bolan's hand as he was introduced.

"Don McRae... Mike Belasko. He's the guy I told you about," Colgan said.

McRae looked Bolan up and down, as if trying to decide whether or not he could take him. His thin lips, compressed into a straight line, gave no hint of what he had decided. Bolan wished he could see McRae's eyes, but they were hidden behind mirrored sunglasses. The bright lenses glinted as McRae bobbed his head up and down. Bolan could almost swear he'd seen the man before, but he couldn't remember where.

"What are you doing out this way, Don?" Colgan asked.

"Just checking things out. We had a woman in earlier to the clinic. She said she saw about a dozen guerrillas along the road here. Thought I better check it out. You know how they are. Anything on wheels is either NPA or army. But, hell, it can't hurt to make sure."

"See anything?"

"Nothin' at all, Tom. I was just getting ready to turn back around when we spotted you. Thought maybe she was right after all." He laughed, but the laugh sounded forced to Bolan, who had taken an immediate dislike to the man.

"I guess maybe we'll go on up the road a ways. How far were you? Not visiting that camp again, were you?"

When Colgan didn't answer, McRae continued. "Tommy, I don't know why in hell you keep going back there. Ain't nothing gonna change if you go a million times. Them people ain't gonna come back. Now you know that. And I know you know, 'cause I told you myself at least a thousand times."

Colgan looked off at the sky. In the quiet, Bolan could hear the wind in the canopy high above, the thick leaves slapping together like the flippers of trained seals. "I'd appreciate it if you'd not be so cavalier, Don." Colgan sounded as if he were caught halfway between rage and sorrow. Another word would tip him one way or the other.

McRae nodded. "All right," he said, waving a hand in disgust, "have it your way."

Colgan turned sharply. "There is no other," he said.

McRae looked at Bolan as if to say the man's a lunatic, but Bolan gave him no sympathy. "Be back in a little while, Tom," he said, still staring at Bolan.

McRae started his engine and backed away from the other jeep, then gunned the engine and bounced onto the road. Bolan watched the jeep disappear without saying anything. Colgan seemed preoccupied, and Carlos tapped the wheel impatiently.

"Señor Colgan," Carlos said, gunning the engine sporadically, "we should go. If Señor McRae is right, we shouldn't be out here."

Colgan turned to look at the young driver, but he said nothing. He just stared as if he were looking right through the jeep, as if it weren't even there.

Bolan took Colgan by the shoulder, but the taller man spun wildly away. "Don't touch me. Don't ever touch me. I don't like it."

Bolan looked at Carlos, who just shrugged. He didn't have to say anything. Bolan shook his head and walked toward the jeep. He climbed into the rear and clicked the safety off his M-16. The whole scene bothered him. Something wasn't right. He didn't know what, but couldn't shake the feeling he would soon find out.

14

Carlos pushed the jeep along in second gear. Over the roaring engine, Bolan could barely hear himself think. He watched the forest on either side of the road, wondering just how perverse Colgan was prepared to be. He wanted to ask the man about Cordero. A sneaking suspicion crept across the back of his skull that Colgan knew more about Harding than he was letting on. And, by extension, that would mean he knew something about Cordero.

Whenever he closed his eyes, Bolan would see the bloody horror that had been made of Frank Henson. Somebody was going to pay for that, and Bolan was dangerously close to not giving a damn who. He would love to take Harding down, then nail Cordero to a tree and send it through a sawmill. But somehow that seemed too easy. It was almost too primitive. The temptation to respond to terror with action more terrible still was seductive, almost as tantalizing as two fingers of Scotch in a clean glass would be to an alcoholic.

Revenge was a drug, and Bolan had succumbed more than once in his life. He was no vengeance junkie, but there was a balance of terror that had nothing to do with nuclear weapons. It had to do with the ways in which human beings were prepared to rend the flesh of their fellows, or split open their bones and smile with the blood running down their chins like cannibals at a feast.

And in the end, it was always the helpless who suffered, who fell before the terrorist's onslaught like wheat to the thresher. It was old women, like those buried in the mound Colgan had shown him. It was children, too young to defend themselves from flies, let alone madmen with automatic rifles. It was the old men whose legs were too frail to walk in the fields, let alone run from the helicopters.

Maybe Colgan was right, Bolan thought. Maybe death could be held at arm's length only by those who were prepared to inflict it on another.

But it seemed, not realism as Colgan characterized it, but anarchism. It was an invitation to every man on the planet to join in combat against every other man. In such a case, there were no winners, just people who hadn't yet lost.

Up ahead a cloud of parrots exploded, distracting Bolan for a moment. He stared at the trees below the horde of colorful birds. Why had they risen up so suddenly, he wondered. Then a glint caught his eye, lower down, among the trees. It flashed once, then again. He shielded his eyes with one hand, then rapped Carlos on the shoulder. The young driver turned, and Bolan jabbed a finger toward the trees. "There's someone in there," he yelled.

Carlos leaned back, and Bolan repeated the warning. This time the driver heard him. He stomped on the pedal, then lifted into third as he gained speed. As they drew near the place where the birds had been, Bolan stared in among the trees. The flash hadn't recurred, but he was convinced someone lay hidden there.

Then, just ahead of them, a huge spout of earth rose straight up, as if a leafless tree had suddenly sprouted fully grown from the earth. As clods of dirt rained down around them, Carlos struggled with the wheel, trying to avoid a gaping hole in the road.

Bolan knew what an exploding mine looked like. He also knew what one could do to a jeep. "Back it up, Carlos," he urged. Colgan turned, as though in a daze, his features suddenly slack. The blue eyes were almost gray and seemed sunken into the skull as if they were retreating. His lips split wide open in a gruesome smile. He hefted his M-16 and jerked the fire control lever onto full-auto.

"Time for a little lesson in realism, Mr. Belasko," he shouted.

Bolan dropped to one knee and fired a short burst from his own rifle. The limitless jungle swallowed the deadly hail as easily as the ocean swallows a few drops of rain. A brief echo of the burst quickly died, and Carlos fought the wheel as the jeep ground its gears and finally allowed him to shift into reverse.

A second mine went off, sending another column of dark earth high into the air. It narrowly missed the jeep, and the concussion slammed into Bolan's body like an invisible fist. The thunderclap made his ears ring.

So far there had been no gunfire from the trees, but it wouldn't be long in coming. As the jeep wove crazily from side to side, Bolan thanked his stars they had been able to avoid the first mine. The plan obviously had been to immobilize them. Whoever was hidden in the dense undergrowth had been hasty, detonating the mine in front instead of behind the jeep. They had blown it and had given their intended target a fighting chance.

Instead of panicking, Carlos used his head, backed off the roadway and slammed the tail of the jeep in between two trees. He jumped down, leaving the engine running. Bolan dove over the side just as the first wave of fire broke over the jeep. Colgan ducked below the dash, then crawled out backward, keeping the jeep between him and the hidden gunmen.

"Can you raise McRae?" Bolan whispered.

Carlos bobbed his head eagerly.

"Do it."

"No," Colgan said, "not yet. We don't need any help."

"We will. And by then, it might be too late."

Carlos watched the two older men. He wanted to call for help, but he didn't want to risk offending Colgan. He seemed in thrall to the doctor, as if under his spell.

"Give me the damn radio," Bolan growled, grabbing for the small transceiver clutched in Carlos's hand. The shiny black box fell to the ground, and Carlos snatched at it, but Bolan was too quick.

"You win." Colgan sighed. "Give it to Carlos. He'll do it."

Carlos reached out to take the small radio and flashed a grateful smile as soon as Colgan had turned away. Bolan crawled toward the front end of the jeep and lay flat on the ground. He slid under the bumper and used the barrel of his M-16 to push away a clump of fern leaves. The firing from the ambush had stopped, and the jungle was quiet except for a nervous whisper as Carlos tried to raise McRae on the radio.

"How much ammunition do you have?" Bolan asked, backing out from under the jeep.

"Three magazines," Colgan said. "And there might be a couple more in the jeep. There's usually a bag under the seat."

Colgan got to one knee alongside the passenger seat and cut loose with a short burst.

"Save it," Bolan barked. "We're outgunned, and you can bet your last dollar they've got plenty of bullets."

"Most of them can't shoot worth a damn," Colgan retorted.

"You don't even know who they are."

"Like hell I don't. It's a bunch of NPA bullies. Sure as I'm sitting here, that's who they are."

"How can you be certain?"

"I've been here a lot longer than you. And if I learned one thing, it's that the NPA couldn't shoot dead fish in a small barrel. If that had been some of Harding's chums in the Brigade, we'd already be small pieces of meat dripping off the leaves on either side of the road. Those guys are well trained. They know how to shoot and they shoot to kill. If they're going to mine the road, they're going to blow the shit out of something. Bang for the buck is something they understand. But the emphasis is on buck. There is no fiscal irresponsibility with those boys. Hell, they're just like Republicans.'' Colgan laughed, and it turned into a maniacal wheeze. His lungs emptied, and he lost control of himself for several seconds.

Carlos crawled up behind Bolan. "Señor McRae is coming," he said. "Ten minutes."

Bolan moved to a position behind the front wheel, then peered over the hood. Two men advanced along the side of the road through the tall grass. Bolan brought his rifle up to rest on the hood. A burst of fire ripped out of the trees and shattered the windshield. Bolan ducked below the jeep as glass clattered onto the hood and cascaded down over the fenders. Hunks of glass fell into his collar, and small slivers stuck to his neck. He shook his head, and more splinters rained out of his hair and glued themselves to his sweaty forehead.

Bolan lay on the ground and crawled into the trees behind the jeep. Using the blocky tail of the vehicle to screen himself from the two point men, he knelt among the trees. Drawing a bead with the M-16, he clicked the fire control onto single shot. Every shell was precious.

The front man was getting careless, and Bolan held his breath, waiting for a clear shot. The man wore a white headband, and Bolan could see it bobbing just below the tips of the tall blades. He fired once, and the man froze, the headband hovering in one spot like an uncertain hummingbird.

Bolan zeroed in on the headband. He squeezed again. The M-16 cracked, and the headband disappeared. He heard a shout, and a flurry of activity in the grass told him he'd found his mark. Bolan held steady, waiting to see what the second man would do. It was difficult to be certain, but from the fractured glimpses he'd caught, the second man looked quite young.

Sliding down into the brush, Bolan started to cut an angle among the trees. If he could get closer, maybe even slide in behind them, he might be able to put a lid on things before they pulled themselves together enough to make a concerted assault.

The ground was damp, and the leaf mulch silent under his feet. The remaining pointman had stopped shouting, and Bolan couldn't tell whether the man had held his position, fallen back or come on ahead. He checked the spot every few seconds, but the angle kept changing and he was no longer sure of the exact location.

Another burst ripped at the jeep, and Bolan watched the sparks fly from the hood. A loud bang signaled a blown tire, and the jeep hunched to one side. Somebody fired back, probably Colgan, and the two positions traded short bursts for several seconds. Colgan was on semiauto, and he had a heavy finger. Bolan hoped he didn't use all his ammo before McRae got there.

Something cracked off to the right, and Bolan froze for a second, then sank down into the undergrowth. A clump of flowers trembled unnaturally, and he held his breath.

He'd almost missed them.

Two men, flat as snakes, slithered over the leaves, pressing themselves under the bushes, just barely brushing a branch here and there. So slowly that he felt as if it would take him forever, Bolan brought his rifle around. Just as he was in position, one of the men, a scarecrow in khaki T-shirt and fatigue pants, sprang up. Bolan noticed the grenade as he squeezed the trigger.

He hit the deck just as the scarecrow pitched over to one side. He heard a scream, and the scarecrow's partner started to run. Tangled in some sort of vine, he tripped and fell.

Bolan covered his head, and the grenade went off with a dull crump, like a firecracker in a big barrel.

Bolan darted through the brush, his rifle ready. The scarcrow lay on his side. Without looking too closely, Bolan knew the man was dead. The bullet hole in his chest was nothing compared to the chopped liver his back had become. Twenty feet away the second man, his feet still snarled in the tenacious vine, lay on his face. Several shrapnel wounds peppered his back. Bolan dropped to one knee and rolled him over.

He was no more than a kid. His eyes stared at Bolan, big as golf balls. His mouth moved awkwardly, and Bolan bent to hear, but there was no sound and the mouth slowly closed. The eyes glazed over as one hand shot out and grabbed Bolan by the wrist. The kid squeezed, and Bolan made no attempt to pull away.

With a soft "oohhh," the mouth moved one last time, the eyes started to glaze over and the hand fell away. Bolan reached out to close the staring eyes with his thumb.

Up the road an intermittent roar drifted through the trees, growing louder and more consistent. Bolan got to his feet and stepped over the tangle of vines, then cocked an ear. The roar had settled into a steady droning now. It had to be McRae's jeep, Bolan thought as he moved deeper into the trees, finishing the curve and starting back in behind the hidden gunmen.

He wondered how many there were. It occurred to him that he might be walking into the middle of a sizable patrol. But something about their tactics made him doubt it. If there had been a large group, they would not have wasted time on subtlety. They would have charged headlong, relying on numbers to make the difference.

As he headed back in the direction of the road, Bolan could hear whispering voices somewhere ahead among the trees. He moved another twenty feet in, then positioned himself behind a thick-trunked rubber tree. He still heard the voices, but he hadn't seen a thing. It was brighter ahead as the growth thinned out and then was broken altogether by the road. The sound of the oncoming jeep had vanished. If it was McRae, he would be with Colgan. If it wasn't, there should have been gunfire.

With a shrug Bolan started firing into the shrubbery. A startled shout kicked off a flurry among the leaves. Bolan waited for return fire, but heard nothing but the rush of bodies headlong through the foliage. He fired twice more, then plunged after the fleeing men. They had the edge, and he knew, even as he struggled, that they were pulling away from him.

Bolan eased up and headed out into the road. He could see Colgan, Carlos and McRae huddled between two jeeps. McRae was waving his arms vehemently as Bolan broke into a run.

15

The three young prisoners cowered in a corner of the room. McRae shoved one of them with the heel of his hand, knocking the frail kid back into the wall.

"No need for that," Bolan said.

"You butt out," McRae snapped, turning to give the big guy yet one more appraising look. "You're a guest here. Guests mind their own business."

"There's no need to be so rough. He's just a kid."

"The kid was carrying an AK. He'd cut your heart out and eat it. So fuck off."

Colgan stood by silently. The tall man had folded his arms across his chest, and Bolan watched the fingers of one hand patting an elbow. Colgan looked as if he were in an empty room. If he were aware of anything going on around him, it left him uninterested.

"Okay, Carlos," McRae said, "chain these little bastards to the wall while I figure out what to do with them."

Colgan turned suddenly and strode toward the door. Bolan followed him. He grabbed the tall man by the arm and spun him around. "What's going on here?" Bolan demanded.

"We've taken prisoners. Nothing more, nothing less."

"And...?"

"And nothing, Mr. Belasko. That's Mr. McRae's department. I don't interfere."

"What usually happens?"

"Ask him...."

Colgan turned away. He paused for the slightest of moments, balanced on the balls of his feet, then walked across the compound to his hut.

Bolan heard the sharp sound of skin on skin, then a moan. He dashed back into the prison hut. One of the prisoners was down on his knees. Even in the dim light, Bolan could see the angry welt just beginning to swell under the kid's left eye.

The kid looked at Bolan. For a second there was a glimmer of contact, as if the kid were trying to tell him something or asking for help. But the glimmer quickly faded, and the kid turned a baleful glare McRae's way. McRae raised his hand again, and Bolan stepped forward, grabbing the raised hand and bending it back against the wrist.

"That's enough, McRae."

"You mother—" McRae ducked under and spun around, releasing the pressure on his wrist. He dropped into a crouch and bulled toward the big guy. Bolan let McRae throw a couple of wild punches, neatly sidestepping each one, then landed a sharp left just under McRae's right eye. McRae stumbled backward, tripping over the kneeling prisoner.

In a flash the kid was on him, trying to wrap his chains around McRae's throat. He missed twice, then butted McRae with his head. This time he succeeded in getting a loop of chain around the larger man's neck. He started to pull it tight, and McRae scrambled to get his fingers in between the bulky links and the flesh of his neck.

The kid was wiry and he was furious. McRae thrashed around on the dirt floor, trying to throw the kid off him, but he was losing control. His eyes started to bulge, and Bolan saw the skin on either side of the chain start to turn bright white. He looked at Carlos, but Carlos either didn't know what to do or had, unconsciously perhaps, chosen sides.

Bolan reached down and hauled the kid to his feet. McRae, still wrapped in the chains, came with him. Bolan grabbed the kid's right arm and jerked it away from the chains. McRae spun free, then lay on the floor, gasping, as the kid searched Bolan's face for some indication whether he had made a mistake or not.

Bolan already knew the answer. McRae was not going to forget this. Not in two lifetimes. He lay there gagging and cursing, his breath coming in quick, sharp gasps. He braced himself with one hand. The other chafed the skin on his neck, now neatly encircled by a bright red impression of the chain. Each link was clearly and deeply etched.

McRae struggled to his feet, still cursing. He turned on Bolan. "Don't think I'm going to thank you, you son of a bitch. If you hadn't stuck your nose in, this wouldn't have happened in the first place."

"Just make sure it doesn't happen again," Bolan hissed. "Next time I'll let him finish."

Bolan left the prison hut. He heard steps and whirled, but it was only Carlos.

"You have made a bad enemy, *señor*," Carlos whispered. Before Bolan could respond, Carlos was in full stride. A moment later he disappeared into his own hut. Bolan crossed the open space slowly, rubbing one hand thoughtfully against a two-day growth of whiskers. Something was dreadfully wrong, and he just couldn't get a fix on it. It was right under his nose, but Colgan was so bizarre that all the usual indications meant something other than he was used to. It was like trying to read a favorite fairy tale translated into an alien language.

He had to get a handle on the place, and on Colgan, before he could even begin to take the next step. He would need Colgan to get to Harding, but he coudn't stand by and watch McRae's vicious behavior. Marisa seemed like the only way to get to Colgan.

Bolan walked to his hut and sat in the doorway, watching the door of the prison hut. McRae came out a few seconds later, glanced at Bolan, then disappeared into his own hut. It was nearly noon. One by one, men started drifting from their huts to the mess hall. A few of them glanced curiously in Bolan's direction, but none of them so much as raised a hand in greeting. Each man carried his automatic rifle slung over his shoulder.

When Marisa and Colgan appeared, Bolan stood and walked across the clearing to meet them. Colgan looked at him curiously but said nothing. Bolan said hello, and Marisa tilted her head slightly before responding.

"You must be hungry, Mr. Belasko."

"Why?"

"Dealing with Mr. McRae always makes me hungry. I assume you and I are alike."

"You think so?"

"Yes, I do."

"I don't...."

"Why's that?"

"Because I wouldn't put up with him. The man is a time bomb just waiting for somebody to set him off."

"He's an enthusiast," Colgan cut in. "He is a passionate man. You of all people should be able to understand that."

"Passion? Not really. Not that kind, anyway."

"What kind *do* you understand?" Marisa smiled while she waited for his answer. "Or should I guess?"

"You'd better guess," Bolan answered.

"Mr. Belasko has a passion for justice, Marisa." Colgan smiled distantly. "He fancies himself some sort of guardian angel."

"What are you going to do with the prisoners, Colgan?"

"Ah, I've struck a nerve, I see. I didn't realize my characterization was so close to the mark."

"What's the answer?"

"It's no concern of yours."

"I'm making it my concern."

"Very noble of you. But Mr. McRae is an old hand. He knows how to handle such things."

Changing tacks, Bolan hesitated for just a second. "Do you know where Charles Harding is?"

"No."

"Do you know where his headquarters is?"

"I'm sure not. Why, do you wish to change sides?"

"I'm not on any side to begin with."

"Oh, but you are. Whether you wish it or not."

"I have to get to Harding."

"Tell me why."

"I think you already know."

"Do you, now? And just what is it I know?"

"Stop playing games. You carry on like some mystical pharaoh. You're no less a petty autocrat than Harding is."

Marisa placed a hand on Colgan's arm. "That's not fair, Mr. Belasko. My husband is trying to help these people, *my* people. He didn't come here to impose his will on them."

"Like Harding, you mean?"

"Yes, like Harding. And like *you*."

"I'm not trying to impose my will on anyone. But Charles Harding has to be stopped. And, just in case you didn't notice, those three kids in that hut are your people, too. Not mine, not Harding's or McRae's. Not even your husband's, Marisa. They're *your* people. And you stand around and watch while an animal like McRae brutalizes them. What's he going to do with them?"

"I have no idea."

"You better get one, lady. You better get one, before it's too late."

"And I suppose you'll clap on your white hat and ride out of the hills to save the world, then ride off into the sunset. Is that it, Belasko? Is that what you have in mind? By God, I misjudged you. You're a fucking *hero*, that's what you are," Colgan said, turning his back. "But this country already has enough heroes."

"And what the hell are you?" Bolan challenged. "What's your scenario for the next fifty years?"

"Don't bait me. You'll be sorry."

"That's exactly how I'd expect a tyrant to react. Don't disagree, don't have an opinion, don't challenge my wisdom, my *authority*."

"You're here by my sufferance. I think you ought to remember that."

"Is that the good doctor speaking? The Philippine answer to Albert Schweitzer? Sufferance? Where the hell do you get off talking to anyone about sufferance? You're not a god, Colgan. You're not even a good doctor. You tolerate an animal like McRae, let him tyrannize helpless prisoners, and you fancy yourself a benefactor, a savior. Is that what you suffer from, Colgan? Do you have a messiah complex?"

Colgan smiled. "Very good, Mr. Belasio. The accused becomes the prosecutor. But you can't wriggle off the hook that easily. It's not simple—life is not simple."

"But you know its secrets, don't you Colgan? You're above it all, up there on Olympus. But you know something? I think the thin air has addled your brain. I think you're losing touch with reality and have become part of the problem. I know it. And so does Marisa."

She recoiled from the challenge as if he had slapped her. She turned away and nearly fell as she reached back toward her hut. Colgan took a deep breath.

"I don't know what you're up to, but I want you out of here."

"But you brought me here, Colgan. Don't you remember?"

"Well, I was wrong. You're not what I thought. You're a mistake, Belasko. A walking anachronism. You don't belong here."

"Neither do you, Colgan."

"Get *out*, damn you!"

"I'm not leaving. Not until you tell me where I can find Charles Harding. And Juan Rizal Cordero."

Bolan was pleased to see Colgan flinch. "So, the name rings a bell, does it?"

"I don't know what you're talking about. I never heard of the man."

"The hell you didn't. You know where he is, where they both are. And you're going to tell me, or I'll beat it out of you."

He stepped toward the taller man and grabbed him by the front of the shirt. Bolan knew he was treading on very thin ice, but he was frustrated. Too many blind alleys. Too much bullshit. Lots of heat and now he wanted some light, damn it. He started to shake Colgan, twisting his grip on the shirt as Colgan tried to pull himself free.

The click of an automatic rifle brought him to his senses. He turned to look over his shoulder and saw Carlos, his rifle in hand, shaking his head.

"Let him go, *señor*."

"Why, Carlos? Why do you stay here? What do you see in this man?"

"He is a good man, *señor*. He cares for my people, for my country."

"He cares only for himself, Carlos. And for the power he has over you."

"He has no power, *señor*. I can leave anytime I choose. Now, let him go. Please..."

Bolan shoved Colgan backward as he let go of the shirt. But the doctor was a lot sturdier than he looked. He staggered a step or two but didn't fall.

"You leave tomorrow morning, Belasko," Colgan said. He turned on his heel and walked away.

Bolan looked at Carlos, shaking his head. "You're making a big mistake, Carlos. The man's insane. He'll drag you down with him if you let him. And make no mistake, he's going to take a fall. A bad one."

"No, *señor*. You're wrong."

"I hope so, for your sake."

16

Bolan stared in amazement. Colgan, dressed in white from
head to foot, bent to duck under the lintel and stepped into
the open. Almost ghostly in the brilliant sunlight, his figure seemed to float over the ground, and he sat in the passenger seat of Carlos's jeep without seeming to climb in.

Marisa sat next to Bolan in the second jeep. "This is my
idea, you know," she said.

"And just what do you hope to gain?" Bolan looked at
her, head cocked to one side. She wore sunglasses that
picked up the sun and glinted small yellow daggers.

"Gain? Why, nothing. I just thought you should see what
my husband is really like. You should see how he treats the
people, how they look up to him."

"Idolize him, do they? Is that what you mean?"

"No." She turned away. "You're like all the others. You
don't think a white man can come to a place like this without either going native or becoming Lord Jim. That's what
Thomas means, you know, by the third way. He wants to be
among the people, not lord it over them or becoming one of
them. He wants them to meet him halfway."

"He has a funny way of showing it. What's the point of
his getup?"

"Getup?"

"The white. He looks like a saint in a bad movie."

"Maybe he is, Mr. Belasko."

"Is that what you think he is? A saint?"

"Perhaps. I know he has done wonders for thousands of people. I know they love him and respect him for what he's done."

"I think your husband is a very dangerous man. He's made some sort of bargain with the devil, and the devil will eat him alive."

"I don't believe in devils, and neither does my husband."

"Do you believe in Charles Harding? Do you believe in Juan Rizal Cordero?"

Marisa didn't answer him immediately. When she finally spoke, Bolan could sense the uncertainty in her, as if she were wrestling with something unpleasant. "You must understand . . . it is difficult here. My husband doesn't want to take sides. But the countryside is in turmoil. The people hate the army, and they don't trust the government. Thomas is walking a very fine line. He tries to stay neutral. The NPA will attack us sometimes, because it is not a single entity. Every group is a law unto itself. Thomas makes no distinctions. If someone needs medical help, he gives it without regard to politics."

"Does that inlcude members of the Leyte Brigade?"

"Yes, it does."

"Then he does know where Harding is, doesn't he?"

Marisa stayed silent.

"Do you understand that Harding and Cordero are planning to destroy this country? They will level it, if they have to, to save it from the NPA. Colgan showed me the village where . . ."

"I know, he told me."

"Has he told you that Manila will look the same way if Harding isn't stopped?"

Marisa fluttered a hand in the air, then waved it vaguely, as if to chase away something neither of them could see. Bolan sighed but said nothing more.

Carlos started his engine, and Bolan's driver followed suit. Together the two jeeps, followed by a truck full of medical equipment, began to roll out of the camp. As they slipped through the entrance to the road, the truck scraping its roof on some low-hanging branches, Bolan glanced back. Behind the truck, a third jeep, this one sporting four heavily armed men, fell in line.

Bolan leaned closer to Marisa. He had to shout to be heard above the roaring engines. "Where are we going?"

"Malanang. There is an epidemic there, probably measles. Thomas has to set up a quarantine hut and innoculate those who haven't already contracted the disease."

"How did you meet Colgan?"

"That's a long story."

"We have time."

"Not now, Mr. Belasko. Maybe some other time."

The road was unusual. For two hours they traveled under the hammering sun, and Bolan saw not a single sign of its construction. It was as if a laser had cut through the forest, incinerating everything in its path and fusing the surface of the road to a smooth, molded contour, running off on either side into a shallow ditch.

Here and there, smaller roads, less precise and not nearly as well maintained, wound off between two hills or stabbed suddenly off among the trees. It was primeval forest face-to-face with man's will to subdue the planet. It seemed to be a stalemate. The road itself seemed free from natural incursion, but twenty feet on either side, jungle as faceless and ancient as any on earth marched off to the mountains.

It was like traveling in a time machine, Bolan thought. He wouldn't have been surprised to round a bend in the road and come face-to-face with a dinosaur. And the thought brought him back to Thomas Colgan—another kind of dinosaur. He was a vestige of the nineteenth century. Maybe he had mastered modern medical science, but his attitude was a hundred years old. What puzzled Bolan was why Marisa didn't see it that way.

Her country was simmering on a low boil, had been for forty years, and yet she seemed not to understand that Colgan was not a solution any more than Marcos had been or Charles Harding threatened to be.

Most likely she was blinded by misplaced gratitude, he thought, unable to see him for what he was because she so much wanted him to be a savior. The road began to slide downhill, now, and Bolan looked back at the gentle rise behind him. As they descended more and more sharply, the forest grew deeper and the trees grew taller. They were heading into the very bowels of Luzon. This was NPA country at its most pristine, a place where the Philippine Army was just a rumor, where civilization consisted of this single road and, more than likely, an arsenal of smuggled weapons.

Far ahead, as the road bottomed out, Bolan saw a flutter of white. He leaned forward to get a better look. As they approached, he recognized it as a white cloth on a stake driven into the ground just off the side of the road. Without having to ask Marisa, he realized it was a sign that had some connection to their journey.

Carlos pulled over about fifty yards before the stake. He climbed down and left the engine running. Colgan stayed in the jeep. Bolan's jeep stopped in the middle of the road, the truck and the third jeep right behind. Bolan watched as Carlos walked slowly toward the flag. The young man hefted his rifle nervously, and his head swiveled constantly from the flag to the trees on either side of the road and back again.

"Maybe I should go with him," Bolan said.

"No! You stay where you are," Marisa snapped. "You're not just a visitor here, you're an intruder."

"And your husband isn't?"

"He was invited."

She said no more. Bolan climbed down to stretch his legs. His spine ached from the jarring of the jeep's tight suspension. It was hard to pin down, but something bothered him about the whole operation. It seemed curiously theatrical, like everything else about Thomas Colgan. But if it was just a dramatic performance, who was the audience for which it was intended, he wondered. Surely Colgan wasn't going to such a lot of effort for his benefit.

And that, of course, he suddenly realized, was the key. Colgan was doing it for *himself*. It was a play in which Colgan was the star and the sole audience. Colgan had constructed an elaborate image, was using the whole world as his stage, and was prepared to give himself rave reviews. It didn't matter what anyone else thought, and it didn't matter whether anyone else even saw the performance. Colgan wanted to please himself, and he had to feed his enormous and eccentric ego.

Bolan knew that such an ego was voracious. Soon even so elaborate a charade as this would not be sufficient. More and more would be necessary. Colgan had bought into the self-constructed myth so totally that he wouldn't be able to see it even if it were pointed out to him. That was why he lost his patience with Bolan, and why he kept everyone, even Marisa, at arm's length.

Let somebody close, and you have to acknowledge their existence. You have to interact, and once that happens, you are forced to realize that the world holds a hell of a lot more than just yourself. For a man like Thomas Colgan, the Filipino people were not people at all. They were props. Their diseases and injuries were part of the script, and they were what enabled him to shine so brightly.

And that's as far as Colgan cared to see. It was as if he lived inside a plastic bubble. People on the outside could see through it, see him gliding on angelic feet, ministering to the sick and infirm. But when he looked back, all he saw was his own reflection on the inside of that bubble. No matter which way he turned, it was his own face he saw. And he liked what he saw too much to ever want to look at anything else.

Carlos had reached the flag and stood with his back to the convoy. Bolan saw him turn sharply to the left, then raise a hand in greeting. A moment later two men in fatigues materialized against the dark green of the jungle. Carlos stepped toward them. One of the men hung back, and the other waded through waist-high grass. He said something to Carlos, who turned and waved, then together they started walking back toward the jeep, accompanied by one man.

Carlos waited for his companion to climb into the jeep, then jumped behind the wheel. He released the emergency brake, and the jeep bumped forward in first gear. As the small convoy rolled slowly ahead, Bolan watched Colgan, who had said nothing to the man and had barely even looked at him. Instead he sat with his hands in his lap, staring straight ahead.

When Carlos reached the flag, the second guide waved him on, running through the tall grass for about fifty yards. He turned left, heading toward the trees, and pulled aside a net interlaced with green fronds. A small lane appeared in the forest wall, and Carlos wrestled the jeep through the shallow ditch and into the tall grass. Bugs swarmed up out of the thick clumps and buzzed around them as they bounced over the uneven ground and into the lane.

After the third jeep had entered the forest, the guide replaced the netting and eased through a narrow gap in the trees. He climbed into Bolan's jeep without saying anything. Carlos jolted ahead now, and they made their way slowly forward. The big truck, its canvas cover slapped incessantly by branches, groaned and squeaked as its chassis twisted back and forth.

Bolan looked at the new passenger, who kept his eyes forward and made no attempt to communicate with the rest of them. The lane snaked its way, tall grass nearly shrouding the hint of ruts beneath. The lane had been cut some time ago, and many of the stumps, cut off just above the soil, had already begun to sprout new shoots, which whipped at the undercarriage of the jeep, slapping against the gas tank and filling the narrow gap with a hollow drumming sound.

The lead jeep braked, its taillights flashing and smearing a wash of artificial color over the shiny green leaves. Carlos leaned forward and the engine died. Bolan's driver turned off his own engine. Behind them the truck continued to rumble.

"We're there," Marisa stated.

"Looks like," Bolan said.

"Watch Thomas. You'll see what I mean."

"He's still sitting in his jeep. Somebody's coming to talk to him, I guess." Bolan waited until a small man in fatigues and a headband, like an aged version of the one who had climbed into their own jeep, halted beside Colgan. The doctor turned his head and leaned down to listen to the new arrival. Bolan was reminded of scenes of the Pope among the faithful.

Colgan climbed down from the jeep, the little old man darting in and out like an anxious child. Colgan moved toward the scattered tents, and children raced toward him on their own or were dragged by stern-faced women in khaki with rifles slung over their shoulders.

The men of the camp seemed to hang back, forming a ragged ring around the growing knot of women and children. Colgan nodded and patted the children on their heads like a man dispensing indulgences rather than medicine. When he reached the center of the camp, towering over the crowd, his white clothes gleaming in the morning sun, he turned and waved toward the medical supply truck. For a moment Bolan held his breath, waiting for a thunderbolt to be summoned by that long, shining arm.

"Maybe now you can begin to see my husband for what he is," Marisa said.

"I already do."

17

Bolan lay on the narrow cot, his arm folded under his head. The moist air smothered him, pressing on his chest like a layer of damp concrete. He had tried to sleep off and on for two hours. His watch told him it was nearly three in the morning, but it made no difference.

In disgust he threw the light blanket off and let his legs dangle down over the edge of the metal frame. He leaned over and tugged on his boots. Rubbing his hands on his thighs, he realized how tight he was. The muscles in his legs felt like metal bands. Getting to his feet with a weary sigh, he stretched his arms out as far as he could, then did a dozen deep knee-bends. His legs loosened up a little, but he could feel the tension sitting there in his gut like a ball of freshly smoked rubber.

He strapped on the AutoMag and walked to the door of the hut. Fitted with a simple screen door, it was bug tight and hot as an oven. Already he could feel a river of sweat coursing down his backbone. He listened to the night with one hand on the doorjamb. A small trickle of sweat ran down his bare forearm, beaded at his elbow, then dripped away.

Outside he could just see the corner hut at the right end of the compound. Just beyond, on the edge of the trees, a small glow told him a bored sentry was taking a smoke to ease the monotony. It always amazed him how predictable men could be. Left alone with the night, even men who had no interest in smoking reached for an open pack, if only to take a puff and crush the nearly whole cigarette under a boot heel. The coil of smoke, at least, moved. It made one feel a little less alone, as if the smoke might somehow be a companion until the next shift.

Deep in the jungle, something screamed. It was frightening, but not a scream of terror. More likely a predator, howling its frustration, was coping with the night in its own fashion. Idly Bolan pushed the screen door away with the toe of one boot. It swung open noiselessly, and almost like an automaton, he stepped out into the thick, hot air.

Stepping aside to let the screen door close behind him, he bumped it with a hip to make sure it shut tightly. Whatever else he accomplished, he didn't want to come back to a room full of mosquitoes. He walked out into the center of the green half-moon that echoed the curve of the line of huts. Looking up, he saw stars brighter than any he'd seen in a long time. Only this far from the city were so many stars visible that one could keep counting them until morning.

A single dim rectangle of light spilled through one of the screen doors. Faintly orange, it came from a kerosene lamp. For purposes of saving fuel, the generator was shut down every night at nine. The day was too insistent very early in the tropics, and no one had the need of electricity much after dark.

He started walking without knowing quite why. Colgan's hut, like the others, was dark. The camp was as quiet as an empty tomb. The cigarette across the compound was long since dark. Staring into the night, Bolan saw no trace of the sentry. Behind him someone moaned, probably having a bad dream. The sound was barely human and sent a shiver up Bolan's spine. The chill lingered long after the sound faded away.

A shadow passed through the center of the light smear, and Bolan knit his brows. Who else, he wondered, would be up at this time of night? And why would they be in the prison hut?

Curious, he started toward the hut when he heard a strangled cry. It sounded as if it had been squeezed off before it really got going. Bolan quickened his pace, checking to make sure the AutoMag was on his hip. The shadow passed through the wedge of light a second time as Bolan drew close.

He reached the door just as a second stillborn cry dribbled to a halt. Bolan leaned forward to peer into the hut, thinking perhaps one of the prisoners had taken sick. He grabbed the door, but it wouldn't open. That was normal, but something bothered him. There was still the matter of the light and the shadow.

Pressing his face against the oblong, barred window, he couldn't make anything out. Then he caught a whiff of something that made his stomach coil back in on itself. He thought for a moment he was going to gag. It was the unmistakable smell of flesh. Burning flesh.

"Anyone in there?" Bolan called.

No one answered, and he twisted himself around to try and squeeze a look, but the bars were just too close together. He noticed a single window, set in the wall directly opposite the door, and he sprinted around to the back of the hut. He wasn't afforded a better view there, but the smell was even stronger.

"Anyone there? What's going on?" He called more loudly this time, but still got no answer.

Bolan raced back to the front door, grabbed the bars and pulled. He propped himself against the door with his feet and put his entire weight behind the pull. His muscles strained as he tried to use himself as a lever to pry the bars free. Twice he lifted himself off the ground and slammed his heels into the door, but the bars held.

He couldn't see the lock on the inside and didn't want to wake the entire camp, but he had to do something. What-

ever was happening inside was dreadful—that much he suspected. Pounding his fist against the door, he heard it echo
hollowly from inside, followed by a faint sound like a
snicker. He called, and again he heard the snicker, like a kid
laughing behind his hands when he's put one over on the
teacher.

Bolan slammed a fist into the door in his anger, but it refused to budge. Feeling along the door's edge, he realized
the design was less than perfect. The hinges, mounted with
the pins facing out, were accessible. Using the butt of the
AutoMag, Bolan rapped on the top pin. It resisted at first,
then started to slide free, a quarter inch at a time.

Hearing footsteps, Bolan turned to see the sentry rushing
toward him, rifle at an angle across his chest.

"What's going on?" the sentry asked.

"You tell me," Bolan said. From inside, there was a sudden hiss, and the stench of burning flesh wafted through the
open bars.

"Give me that," Bolan snapped, indicating the survival
knife sheathed on the sentry's hip. The man looked puzzled, but Bolan ignored the look and snatched the knife
from its sheath. Dropping to one knee, he pried the lower
pin loose enough to get the fat edge of the blade under it.
Using it like a crowbar, Bolan worked the knife up, slid it
farther along, lifted again, then placed the fat edge flat
against the pin, just under its head. He tugged up, and the
pin shot free. He repeated the process on the second hinge,
then snapped the already loosened pin out of the top hinge.

Again he grabbed the bars and pulled. This time, pivoting on the latch, the door swung open. Bolan pushed it
aside, where it hung at a crazy angle. He stepped through
the door into a wash of orange light. In one corner McRae
sat on a chair, his eyes a little glazed, a bottle of Scotch in
his lap.

On a table next to him, the open flame of a kerosene lamp
flickered in an occasional draft. A survival knife projected

from the wall behind McRae. It started to tilt downward slowly, then dropped with a faint ping as it stuck into the floor point-first. An elaborate ivory inlay in the handle caught fragments of light and splashed them on the floor in tiny pools.

"What's going on here?" Bolan demanded.

McRae chuckled. "Just cooking up a little trouble for the NPA," he said.

Bolan looked at the three prisoners, who lay motionlessly huddled next to the wall like bundles of rags. He dropped to his knees beside the nearest prisoner. He shook the young man, but knew already that it was pointless. The skin was cold to the touch. The shirt felt sticky to his touch, and he leaned forward to find it soaked with blood. He rolled the kid over, and noticed a series of ragged, blackedged burns on his cheeks, like steps running up from the jawbone and stopping just under the right eye.

Bolan took the kid's jaw in his hands and turned the head to look at the other cheek. A similar pattern, like some bizarre tribal marking, lined that cheek also. A knotted rag bulged behind the kid's teeth. That would explain the strangled cries.

Bolan stared in disbelief and deep rage tightened his jaw.

Quickly he checked the second prisoner. That one, too, choked on a knotted rag. The burn marks were on his chest, where the shirt had been sliced up the middle. Darkening blood from a gaping throat wound concealed half of the burns.

Just to confirm what he already knew, Bolan examined the third boy and found what he'd expected. Bolan turned to stare at McRae, and there was a deadly calm on his face. "You'll be sorry you did this."

"Hey, man, I got to know what they know. I got responsibilities. Man won't talk, you got to make him."

"Responsibilities?" Bolan shouted as he threw himself across the hut. McRae tried to avoid the charge, but managed only to slip off the chair and land in a heap on the floor beside it.

Bolan grabbed him by the shirt and hauled him to his feet. He swung his fist into the man's midsection. McRae doubled over and flew backward into the wall. As Bolan was reaching for him, McRae swung an arm up and chuckled. "Uh-huh. Just hold it."

He held an ugly Colt .45. Behind the gun, his face split in a triumphant grin. "Tut, tut, big boy, you just fucked up. I knew you would."

Boaln made a slight move, and McRae moved the automatic back and forth. Using one hand to hold himself erect, he ratcheted himself up the wall with his hips, dropped into the chair again, then called out.

"Take Mr. Belasko's gun, Juanito."

Bolan looked at the sentry, who was still staring at the three crumpled bodies against the wall.

"Juanito? I'm waiting... Do it, or I'll blow your fucking brains all over the wall."

Juanito looked at Bolan as if asking for his approval. Bolan said nothing. The guard stepped close and wrapped his fingers around the butt of Bolan's pistol, then backed away.

"You watch him now, Juanito, you hear me?" McRae knelt down to retrieve the chains that were locked around the dead bodies.

When the chain was free, McRae got to his feet and moved past Bolan, keeping his distance. Slipping up behind Juanito, he darted forward, swinging his Colt in a vicious arc. The blow caught Bolan over the right ear, and he went down hard. McRae kicked him in the small of the back, then snapped the chains around Bolan's ankles and secured it through the bolts. He slipped a pair of handcuffs from a pants pocket and clicked them shut, pinning Bolan's arms behind his back.

He towered above his captive. "You won't be going anywhere," he snarled. "'Cause I got somebody wants to talk to you, but after he does, I'm gonna decorate you some."

McRae looked at Juanito. "I'll be back later." Then, pointing to the three corpses, he said, "In the meantime, put out the garbage."

18

By nightfall of the following day, Bolan began to wonder. The day had dragged on, and he'd kept watching for McRae to come. Hot, wet air, thick as steam, had choked Bolan as he tried to formulate a plan. The camp had fallen strangely silent in the late afternoon. As it continued to grow darker, the silence grew deeper. Finally he heard a key in the lock.

Bolan crouched in the corner. The key continued to grind in the lock as he steeled himself. Clenching his fists, he stared at the door, balancing on the balls of his feet. He heard the latch fall away and slap against the wooden frame. Then the hinges squeaked, and the small block of dim, barred gray was replaced by a tall oblong just as gray and featureless.

Bolan gathered the chains in a loose coil, muffling them as best he could and giving himself all the slack he could find. If everything worked, he would be able to come within five feet of the door. It was just a matter of timing. He had already started toward the opening when the outline of a figure detached itself from the gray mass. Bolan held himself back, but the figure heard something and hissed sharply. The head turned, and Bolan recognized Marisa.

She raised one hand and called, "Psst...Mr. Belasko..."

"Here," he called in a low voice just as a second shadow blocked the doorway.

He thought for a second she had set him up, but Carlos ducked inside and pulled the door closed. "Hurry, Señora Colgan," he whispered.

Marisa slithered over to Bolan's side, and he heard the tiny sound of a small key against case-hardened steel. The lock on his shackles opened, and he eased the chain to the ground. Then she grabbed his arm, as he presented his cuffed hands. When the cuffs snapped open, he felt confused.

"What's going on?" Bolan asked.

"No time for questions. Here, put these on." She handed him a shapeless bundle. But even in the darkness, his fingers recognized the butt of the AutoMag. He slipped the sling over his shoulders, then unfolded the Beretta's harness and shrugged it on, as well.

"Ready?" Carlos asked.

"All set," Bolan said. "Where to?"

"Come..." It was all Marisa said, but there was a new quality to her voice. She seemed uncertain, as if something had happened to tilt her world out of kilter.

Bolan took her hand and moved to the door. She kept close to him, as though she could find some reassurance. Carlos stepped through first, darting into the shadows. Bolan went out and followed Carlos around the corner and into the darkness alongside the hut. Overhead the stars sparkled and something opaque swerved like a drunken kite, then vanished into the trees.

He nearly knocked Carlos down as he swept around the second corner. Carlos held a finger to his lips and waved for Bolan to follow suit, then sprinted into the bush. Bolan plunged after him, tugging Marisa more firmly, half hauling her through the tangled growth. Carlos used the trees as a shield as he circled behind the full length of the compound then halted on the edge of a small clearing.

Bolan saw the jeep squatting there in the darkness. An M-60 machine gun was mounted in the rear. Now Bolan took the lead. He dashed into the open and swiftly helped Marisa into the passenger seat. Carlos scrambled behind the wheel as Bolan climbed over the tail and knelt beside the M-60.

Carlos turned the key, and the engine sputtered for a second before catching. Marisa got up from the seat, her hands groping for the side of the jeep as Carlos floored it. She lurched to one side. Bolan thought for a moment she had fallen. Momentarily stunned, he realized she was trying to climb out.

"No, no, no," she said, her voice beginning to break as it climbed in pitch and volume. "I can't. I can't leave."

Bolan snaked an arm around her waist and hauled her back. He plopped her firmly into the seat as Carlos swung out of the clearing and bounced through a thin stand of trees.

The jeep rattled through a trench, rose at a steep angle as its left wheels climbed along the length of a fallen tree, then fell with a sickening jolt as it slid off.

Marisa still struggled to pull free of Bolan's grasp, but her writhing gradually stopped. She slumped forward, her head on her chest, and her shoulders shook. Carlos reached over to pat her, then withdrew his hand as the jeep started to fight against him again.

A moment later they were free. The jeep bounced through another ditch and gained the road. Bolan looked behind, but everything seemed as dark and quiet as before. Carlos settled down and let the engine drop from a full-throated roar to a steady rumble. He kept looking over his shoulder as if he couldn't believe they hadn't been followed.

Marisa continued to collapse in on herself. She seemed to shrink in the seat as though dissolving in her own tears. Bolan kept one hand on her shoulder to provide her with reassuring human contact.

They drove without headlights, Carlos leaning forward now to see the road as well as he could. The yellow beige of the clay surface looked like a washed-out brown under the starlight. It snaked ahead of them, but the jeep held steady and Carlos began to relax a little. Four or five miles from the camp, Bolan tapped him on the shoulder.

"Pull over," he said.

Carlos turned to look at him as if he'd just been asked to do the impossible. He glanced at Marisa, but she was still lost in herself. She either hadn't heard Bolan's command or didn't care enough to object. Carlos shrugged, threw the transmission into neutral and coasted until he found a small open area off the left side of the road. The jeep rolled to a halt as branches began to scrape at its undercarriage.

"Now," Bolan said, "what's going on?"

Carlos shrugged again. "We had to leave, *señor*."

"Why?"

Carlos looked at Marisa again. Clearly he was waiting to see if she'd object to an answer. When she didn't say anything, he sighed. "Señor McRae..."

"What about him?"

"Señora Colgan ... she heard him talking."

"Spit it out, Carlos. What did she hear?"

"He was talking about you, *señor*. And he said...he was going to kill you, just like he did the boys. Only slower."

Bolan nodded. That figured. But why had Marisa intervened? And where had Colgan been while that had been going on?

"And Señora Colgan objected, is that it?"

"*Si, señor*, and Señor Colgan, too. He objected, too."

"And what did McRae do?"

"Nothing, *señor*. He left, that's all I know."

"Where did he go?"

"I don't know."

"Did anyone leave with him?"

"*Si, señor*. Three or four, maybe more. But I don't know where they went."

"Does anyone else know? Any of the other men?"

"I don't know, *señor*. I don't know anything more than I just told you."

Marisa stirred in her seat, and Bolan thought she was going to say something, but she just curled up and continued to shake. It was a noiseless tremor. Her whole body quivered as if she were inhabited by a silent motor.

"What about Señor Colgan? Where is he?"

"He went after Señor McRae..."

"Alone?"

"With two men. He took guns and he went. He didn't say when he would be back."

"Why did he go after McRae?"

Carlos shrugged and spread his hands in a helpless gesture.

Marisa unwound slowly, like a flower blooming in stop-action photography. She turned to Bolan but said nothing at first. In the darkness Bolan couldn't see her face very well, and he was grateful.

After swallowing hard, she started to speak hesitantly. "He accidentally found out something about McRae," she said. Her voice was cold, remote as the moon. "I don't know what it was."

"Didn't he say anything?"

"He was in a rage. Whatever it was, it must have been terrible. He said McRae was a traitor, that he had betrayed him and that he had to be stopped."

"Stopped from what?"

"I don't know."

"Did he say where McRae had gone? Anything that would tell us where to look?"

"We can't do that. McRae will kill you. He has several men with him. I don't know how many, but he was probably going to meet up with others. Who knows how many they could be? What can we do?"

"We can try to find your husband. He's not safe with McRae."

"McRae wouldn't dare hurt him. Thomas is frightful when he's angry, but he's not afraid of anyone or anything."

Bolan bent close to her, looking into her eyes intently. "Marisa, stop lying. If you know anything, you better tell me now."

She wrenched her head away. "There is nothing to tell."

"Your husband's life is at stake. He's gone after Harding, hasn't he? He knows where to find the man. And that's where McRae went, too, isn't it?"

"No!"

"Tell me!"

"I don't know, damn you, I don't know." She jumped from the jeep and started to run. Within a half dozen steps, her feet became entangled in a vine, and she fell heavily. Bolan raced to her, but she kicked at him and rolled on her back. He caught one hand, then the other.

"Leave me alone."

"I just can't do that."

"It's your fault. All your fault. If you hadn't come here, none of this would have happened."

"I didn't come of my own free will. You know that, and you know why. That's more than I know. Now tell me what I want to know. Come on, Marisa, there's no time."

"He...he found out that McRae was working with the Leyte Brigade. They were going to attack the NPA camp we visited the other day. McRae was using Thomas, sabotaging everything he tried to do. Learning the location of NPA camps and passing them along to Harding."

"And what about Cordero? What do you know about him?"

"Nothing. He was here once, that's all."

"What do you know about Harding's plans to terrorize Manila?"

"Only that...Thomas said maybe something like that would happen. He was arguing with McRae and I overheard them. But it was a while ago, before Thomas learned what he later found. He, Thomas…that's got nothing to do with him. That's Harding.''

"What else?"

"That's it, I swear..."

Bolan stared at her, struck dumb. He looked at Carlos, and thought of the three monkeys.

He knew which one he was.

19

Bolan leaned against the front fender of the jeep. Behind him, Marisa and Carlos conversed in hoarse whispers. She had asked for a chance to talk to Carlos alone, and Bolan, hopeful that she would see just how limited her options were, had agreed.

The sounds of the night began to change as the sky started to brighten. The night creatures gradually settled into their burrows or found places to sleep high in the canopy. It was too early yet for the day shift, but it wouldn't be long. The whispers lost their intensity behind him, and Bolan sensed that Marisa had come to some agreement with Carlos. What it might be, he would soon find out.

The deep blue-black velvet turned milky gray, like a charcoal wash. The stars died away one by one, and the horizon began to sharpen; a white line, tinged with red, like a taut wire stretched from peak to peak along the Sierra Madre range. It looked as if the ocean had burst into flame and a tidal wave of molten color were sweeping across the trackless Pacific.

Then, so suddenly he couldn't believe it could be so silent, the sun appeared, a brilliant red mound in the east, and the sky caught fire. Far to the east, wispy red clouds, like huge pennants fluttering in impossibly slow motion, turned pink and bleached before his eyes.

He heard Marisa's soft approach. She placed a hand on his shoulder. "Mr. Belasko," she whispered, "you're right." He turned to her with a sober look.

"We have to hurry, Señor Belasko," Carlos said, climbing into the jeep. When Bolan and Marisa climbed in, he started the engine.

Bolan sat on the jump seat beside the M-60. He let one arm dangle over the big machine gun as the jeep lurched into the road. Directly ahead, the sky was wall-to-wall red. Then, as if someone had changed a filter, it turned orange. By the time they had gone a hundred yards, the orange had faded to yellow. Morning was getting started in earnest, and Bolan felt as if something had changed. The world was somehow a different place. Overnight the script had been rewritten, and he felt as if his part had been expanded. A warning tingled down his spine. Such a change could mean only one thing.

And he didn't want to think about what that might be.

The jungle came alive as they passed, and Bolan had the sense that he was being watched. On the opposite side of the jeep, he spotted a pair of wooden crates banded with galvanized metal strips. He reached around the gun, pulled the top crate off its companion and scraped it along the floor of the jeep.

Marisa turned toward the sound as though she wanted to know what he was doing. He was thankful she didn't seem to notice the belt of ammunition as he grabbed the end and tugged it free. He locked it down with a sharp click, and Marisa nodded as if she had heard the sound before. She turned back to the front without saying anything, her head tilted at that odd angle he had grown used to.

"Carlos," he shouted, "can you find the camp we visited the other day?"

Carlos nodded. *"Si,"* he shouted. "I know where it is."

"Is there any place we can leave Mrs. Colgan?"

Carlos shook his head. "No, *señor*. No place..."

Bolan let that sink in, watching Marisa to see what her reaction might be. She might as well have been made of stone for all the emotion she showed.

Bolan took the M-16 from a rack against the sidewall of the jeep and balanced it across his knees. The fire control lever was on full-auto, and he adjusted it to semi, then took off the safety. Four clips jutted out of a plastic canister suspended from the rack. He stuffed two of them into his shirt pocket and tucked the other pair into the back pocket of his pants.

Something told him he was going to need all the hardware he could carry before the day was out. He recognized the terrain. If memory served, they were only a mile or so from the turnoff to the NPA camp.

Bolan surveyed the tree line to the left, his eye drawn by something that had registered without really being seen. His ears perked up, and he heard the cry of frightened birds. Like a rolling wave, a cloud of parrots pulsed for a moment above the trees, then sank again. It must have been the birds he'd registered before.

As he watched, it rose again, this time higher, then seemed to fracture. The birds fluttered like scraps of bright confetti, then sank down out of sight. As they disappeared, their excited cries swept across the canopy before dying away. And in the echo, he heard another, unnatural sound. Felt it, really, as the floorboard of the jeep picked up the throbbing, vibrating in sympathy.

The pulse grew stronger, and his body reacted to it. Automatically he draped an arm over the M-60. The pulse grew stronger, and he could hear it now, too. A deep throbbing, fading away then coming back even stronger, it seemed to gather more and more strength each time it ceased. And he didn't have to see its source to know what it was. A Huey, somewhere off to the left, had climbed above the trees and had started toward them.

It spelled trouble to Bolan.

The NPA camp had been almost Stone Age in its simplicity. Automatic weapons, yes. But there had been only two vehicles, both in desperate need of repair. They had little fuel to speak of. The idea that they commanded a chopper was unthinkable. Only two options suggested themselves. It was either a Philippine Army ship or it belonged to the Leyte Brigade.

The pulse fractured now, and he realized there were at least two birds, The strange inconsistency of the sound was created by the overlapping rhythm of the two engines, a rhythm that changed constantly as the ships changed speed and their respective distances from him changed along with it. One, from the sound of it, was moving away, heading south. The other seemed to be coming their way.

"Carlos," Bolan shouted, "pull off the road."

Carlos swiveled around. When he saw Bolan pointing at the sky, he nodded that he understood. The jeep veered suddenly, jolting Marisa. She turned to Bolan. "What's happening?" she shouted. "Why are we leaving the road?"

"Helicopters," Bolan yelled in her ears. "At least two, maybe more. If they're army, they might take us for NPA, and if they're not—"

He didn't have to tell Marisa what that would mean.

The chopper roared closer. It was still too far away to see, probably keeping low, just above the trees. Unlike in Vietnam, it had little to fear flying so close to the ground here. The NPA had nothing much beyond small arms, and most of its widely scattered units were no match in firepower for a single Huey carrying the usual complement of guns and possibly rockets.

Carlos wrestled the jeep's steering wheel, struggling to get under the trees. If they were out of sight, they should be all right, since the chopper had no particular reason to be looking for them.

The bushes began to close around the nose of the jeep just as the chopper appeared overhead, sudden as a wasp. It roared past, and Bolan thought for a moment they hadn't been seen, but the Huey slowed, banked in a tight circle and hovered over the middle of the road about four hundred yards past them.

"Get out," Bolan shouted. "They spotted us."

He pushed Marisa down to Carlos, who struggled through the dense undergrowth, hacking at it with a machete to cut a narrow swath for the two of them to slip through. Carlos looked back and Bolan waved him on. "Keep going!"

The chopper pilot seemed to be debating what to do. The big bird hung there in the air. Its engine was a dull undercurrent under the steady whomping of the huge rotor blades. It was side-on, and Bolan spotted two men in the open door. A Browning M-3, a half-inch machine gun on a pintle, was starkly outlined against the bright sky through the open belly of the aircraft.

Bolan swung the M-60 around and made sure the safety was off. He didn't want to waste time on a fight, but it didn't look as if the chopper was going to give him a choice. As near as he could tell, the M-3 was the only armament, other than whatever small arms the crew and passengers might have.

Worse than an attack was the possibility that the chopper might dispatch a ground unit or call in additional support from the other chopper. Shaking his head, Bolan rubbed the sweat beading on his forehead with the back of his hand. The chopper suddenly rose straight in the air, climbing nearly five hundred feet before pivoting on its rotor shaft and swooping toward him at an acute downward angle.

The big bird roared overhead, not more than seventy feet above him, and immediately swung broadside. The door gunner cut loose, and a swarm of half-inch hornets ripped at the leaves just behind him. The gunner swiveled the muzzle down a little, and the pilot tried to steady the bird. Bolan opened up with the M-60, raking the side of the Huey with a short burst until the chopper climbed an invisible wire. It looked like a spider climbing a filament or some ghastly yo-yo abruptly called up to a hidden hand.

Bolan cut loose again with a short burst, but other than a few stray sparks from one strut, he did no damage. The door gunner seemed unused to his weapon and swept the muzzle too far around. His next hail ripped chunks of clay from the road surface, scattering Bolan and the jeep with blobs of soil as sticky as putty. They flattened against the windshield of the jeep, then fell away, leaving round blotches on the glass.

The pilot, realizing his gunner needed help, urged the chopper down, keeping it broadside for a moment, then pivoting again until just the barrel of the M-3 was visible in the open door. Bolan raked the nose and was rewarded with a spiral web of brilliant white cracks in the bubble. The glass was tough and refused to shatter.

Bolan dropped his aim and chewed at the undercarriage. One strut came loose and dangled from a single bolt. It flapped in the rotor wash, then began to swing in a strange circle as the chopper changed its tack again. A couple of men had joined the door gunner, and Bolan could see the barrels of two assault rifles braced against the floor of the chopper. The pilot angled his ship over, and all three guns opened up.

The distinctive pop of a rifle grenade sent Bolan diving over the tail of the jeep into the bushes. The grenade went off with a dull thud, and more dirt cascaded down over him. Bolan got to his feet and dodged into the trees, then cut back. He dove under the layer of bright green and wormed his way back, waiting for the chopper to sweep by, looking for him.

When the engine grew louder, then died away, he saw the antitorque rotor glinting in the sunlight as the Huey passed by. Slipping backward toward the jeep, Bolan hurled himself over the tailgate and swung the M-60 a hundred and eighty degrees. It was his only chance. If he didn't nail the bastard, he might not get another one.

Tugging a length of the ammo belt free to make sure there were no snags, he started hammering. The big 7.62 mm bucked in his hands. He could feel its chatter in his bones from his knees on the floorboard right up through the top of his head. The door gunner, caught by surprise by a burst from behind as the chopper hovered to regroup, pitched forward and out the open door.

Bolan watched the ungainly swan dive with grim satisfaction, then hacked away at the tail. The pilot suddenly realized what was happening and started to climb. Plumes of smoke, probably a ruptured oil line, spewed out a ragged line of holes in the fuselage. The antitorque rotor suddenly stuttered, one shattered blade arcing off like a shiny comet. The imbalance tore its companion to pieces. With stability gone, the chopper began to spin. The pilot tried to adjust, but he was helpless.

The smoke suddenly spouted flame, and Bolan banged away at it, trying to widen the fissures in the fuselage. A moment more, and it was all gone. A huge bright flower bloomed and died in seconds, leaving a black smudge on the blue sky and shattered pieces arcing away in every direction. The shiny metal flashed again and again as it tumbled down. The orange light was gone. The junk had all landed.

Only a round black ball rolled away toward the ocean. Bolan was conscious of his breath scratching at his throat, and the pounding of his heart, like a huge drum, echoed in his ears.

One down.

Then the second bird swooped down, its engine masked by the rumble of the burning ship. Bolan braced for a second assault, but the new bird just roared off, following the highway. For one instant, in the open door, he glimpsed an uninterested onlooker. It was Charles Harding. And he was smiling.

20

Bolan called out to Carlos. His voice disappeared into the jungle. A few squawking parrots answered him, and then silence descended. Bolan snatched the M-16 from the hood of the jeep and moved into the trees. He repeated the summons, and again his voice was swallowed by the trees.

Finally the response came. The call was distant, and Bolan turned to the left. Making a megaphone of his hands, he called a third time. Carlos answered again, sounding a little closer. Bolan waited impatiently until the young man's slender figure parted a stand of tall grass. Slipping through sideways, kicking up a swarm of black flies, the driver tugged Marisa after him. She stumbled, digging her heels in and trying to hold him back.

Bolan ran to them and gently got hold of her by the shoulders. As she crumpled like a baby, he noticed the blood on her arm.

Carlos nodded. "A stray bullet, *señor*, right away."

"Put me down," Marisa screamed. "I don't want to go."

"Stop acting like a child," Bolan snapped. He let Carlos push the brush away and half carried the wounded woman to the jeep, where he set her in the passenger seat.

"First-aid kit?" he asked.

Carlos reached under the front seat for a small, blue plastic box. He fumbled with the latch, then spilled half its contents on the ground as the lid popped unexpectedly. Bo-

Ian turned back to Marisa while Carlos gathered the dropped supplies.

Tearing the sleeve up from the cuff, Bolan exposed the wound. It still oozed blood but didn't appear to be serious. "You're lucky," he said reassuringly. "It didn't hit an artery." She started to pull her arm away, but Bolan held on while he rummaged in the box on the dash.

He poured an antiseptic liquid on the wound, and she inhaled sharply.

"Give me one those green packets, Carlos," Bolan said, spotting some plastic bags of sulfa powder. "Tear it open...."

Carlos handed him the small packet, and Bolan dusted the wound, emptying the bag and handing it back. Applying a pad of gauze, he held it in place with a thumb. Carlos gave him a roll of gauze ribbon, and he wound it around the arm several times. He tore the end with his teeth, tucked it in and let go. Taking a roll of adhesive tape, he tore three long strips, wrapped them over the gauze and patted the ends tight.

Marisa gritted her teeth as Bolan worked, but she no longer struggled to pull her arm free. He looked in the box again, found a plastic bottle of ampicillin and tilted two capsules into his palm.

"Can you swallow pills without water?" he asked.

She nodded, and he gave her the capsules. "One at a time," he warned. When she'd swallowed the antibiotic, Bolan closed the box and handed it back to Carlos.

"Let's get going."

"Where, *señor*?"

"The same place we were going before."

The young man looked unconvinced, and Bolan gave him a commanding look. "We have to find Dr. Colgan and help him if we can."

Carlos shook his head. "Leyte Brigade, *señor*. There is nothing we can do."

"We have to try."

Carlos stared at him. His lips quivered, then he pointed to Marisa, shaking his head. Bolan understood, but pointed up the road. "Drive," he said.

Carlos shrugged. "Whatever you say."

The jeep was battered but still serviceable. It turned over immediately, and Carlos backed toward the road, the transmission snarling as the jeep lurched over the log then sank into the ditch. It stuttered back onto the road. The smooth surface was now pocked and pitted from the M-3, small craters in ragged strips running from side to side. Clots of damp clay lay scattered everywhere.

Carlos let the engine idle for a moment in neutral. "They have jeeps too, *señor*," he said, stabbing a finger into the air.

"Carlos, we don't have a choice."

The driver sighed as he reached for the gearshift. He looked over his shoulder silently, as if to give this crazy man one more chance to come to his senses. Bolan just nodded a forceful directive, and Carlos muscled the jeep into first and let the clutch out slowly. The jeep started to roll as Bolan popped the second box of M-60 ammo open.

Carlos was right, of course. The Leyte Brigade probably did have jeeps, and they might very well have attacked on the ground as well as from the air. It was a chance they'd have to take. There was no percentage sitting where they were, and going back to Colgan's compound would serve no purpose. Carlos had warned them by radio, and they would have to take their chances. What else could they do, Bolan thought, but plunge straight ahead.

Bolan sat on the tail, the M-60 swiveled forward. With a foot he pulled the second ammo crate closer. Chewing his lower lip, he watched the road ahead. If they were going to get any warning, it would be visual. It was difficult to hear anything over the sound of their own engine. They had gone just two hundred yards when Carlos pointed.

Dead ahead, another hundred yards down the road, a bundle of rags lay across the center of the road. Even from this distance, Bolan caught the glint of sunlight on the bright red smear at the front edge of the bundle. Bolan swung the M-60 around, all ready for whatever happened.

But they had nothing to worry about. As they narrowed the distance, Bolan realized the bundle was neither a threat nor a trap. The door gunner, his body smashed and broken from the fall, could do them no harm.

Carlos edged around the corpse, glancing at it with an expressionless face. It was no more to him than a fallen tree, a stone in the road. Then the jeep slowed, and Carlos leaned over. Bolan thought for a moment it was just to get a closer look. But Carlos bent way out over the running board and spat.

They were close now. Bolan scanned the left side of the road. He knew the white flag would no longer be there, but he hoped he could spot the camouflage netting. It couldn't be more than a half mile more. But the tree line was featureless and deceptive, teasing him with a familiar clump of trees, a dead trunk at an angle, then repeating the tease thirty yards beyond. The wall of the jungle started to look like a repeating pattern, as if it were no more than a flat wall artfully disguised with overlapping strips of patterned paper. The jungle, in its infinite variety, was all of a piece. It looked the same in every direction.

Bolan was getting impatient. He was about to lean forward to ask Carlos something when he spotted the netting, ripped aside and hanging like an old rag from only one end. Carlos saw it a moment later and let the jeep roll to a halt.

"No helicopter did that, *señor*," he said, pointing.

"Go ahead, Carlos."

The driver reached down to the floor and pulled his own M-16 closer. Bolan saw him shiver, and felt the chill run down his own spine, too. The jeep started up again as Marisa groaned in her seat. She was only semiconscious, and

Bolan debated the wisdom of leaving her at the entrance. But he realized she would be no safer there.

They rolled into the approach, Carlos letting the gears pulse a little, giving the engine just enough gas to keep from stalling.

Bolan could smell smoke, and it hung in the air like a fine haze. Nothing was visible over the trees, and it seemed odd, until he remembered the camp had very little to burn. A few tents had been the total shelter. The tang of burnt canvas grew sharper as they approached, but the air stayed relatively clear.

He hadn't seen a sign of life yet. They were fifty yards from the open when Bolan asked Carlos to stop. "You stay here with Mrs. Colgan," Bolan said, jumping down.

"Shouldn't I come with you?"

"No. Turn the jeep around and get ready to make a run for it if anything happens."

Carlos waited for Bolan to slip into the trees, then struggled in the narrow alley to get the jeep turned. Bolan stayed just inside the first line of trees, where the undergrowth was thin enough for him to move without obstruction. It was hot, and the bugs swirled around him, small shiny flies like fiery jewels burning his skin when they landed, then darting away ahead of his slapping palm. As he drew closer, he ignored the burning sensation.

A thin plume of smoke, almost white and vanishing no more than fifty feet in the air, was the only thing moving in the open space ahead. Bolan shifted the rifle, spinning it to use the butt to push branches aside. He still couldn't see anything on the ground, and he strained his ears for the slightest sound. Behind him, its pulse nearly inaudible, he heard the jeep engine.

Ten yards from the edge of the trees, he saw the first evidence. The tents were gone, reduced to crumpled heaps, except for the one still burning. A thick black cloud hung almost motionless above it. Too low to be seen over the trees, the cloud spread out as if pressing against an invisible ceiling, trailing off to gray wisps at its edges.

Bolan shinnied up a tree, digging his toes into the rough bark. He could survey the whole camp from twenty feet in the air. Stinging ants scurried over his hands and down into his shirtsleeves, but he ignored them. The campsite, its grass long since trampled flat and yellowed, looked like a moonscape. Craters, probably from aerial rockets and grenades, some interlocking into figure 8s scooped out of the dark soil, pitted the clearing.

The scene was littered with debris, and he could count more than two dozen bodies without even looking carefully. The bodies were in various states of dress, as if whatever had happened had happened early and quickly. From the looks of things, the people had been hit with no warning. They hadn't even had time to grab their weapons. Two tangles of stacked rifles, like broken Tinker-toys, lay in the center of the clearing.

Bolan slipped down the tree and sprinted the last thirty feet to the open ground. Moving cautiously, he scanned the edge of the jungle forty yards across the clearing. He spotted two jeeps that were almost hidden on the far side. One of them had to be Colgan's, but he couldn't explain the other. As he moved toward the center of the camp, he stared in disbelief at the carnage. Men, women and children lay sprawled in the undignified postures of sudden death. Bloodstained clothing, still only half on, trailed away from the bodies, and the buzzing of flies sawed at the air. As he neared a body, the flies would rise up for an instant, then settle back down like a glistening shroud.

He knelt beside the body of a child not more than four. Naked, it lay facedown, a gaping exit wound almost dead center in its back. Bolan shook his head and reached for a tattered blanket lying halfway between the dead child and a woman, possibly the child's mother. A corner of the blanket was curled in her fist, and her hand and arm moved grotesquely as Bolan pulled it free then spread the blanket over the child's body.

Swallowing hard, he moved from body to body, looking for signs of life. Most of the wounds he saw were clearly fatal. The camp was deathly still and silent. The stench of voided bowels hung in the air, mingling with the sharp smell of burning cloth.

An engine exploded into life, and Bolan turned instantly toward the two jeeps. One lurched drunkenly for a second, then snarled toward him. Its tires kicked up clots of mud as the jeep raced straight across the clearing. It bounced once over a broken body, and the driver, bent low behind the wheel, bore down on Bolan as if he wanted to run him over. Bolan swung the M-16 up and fired three quick shots. The jeep's windshield disappeared, but the driver's face was still there, just visible above the wheel, his knuckles white on the black plastic.

Bolan dove to the left, and the driver spun the wheel. He reached through the windshield frame, a .45 in one fist, and emptied the clip at Bolan's rolling body.

The jeep thundered past, and Bolan rolled over once more, bringing the M-16 around and cutting loose. He aimed low, just above ground level. He wanted the bastard alive, if possible. Somebody had to tell him what the hell had happened there. The left rear tire blew out, then the right, but the jeep churned on, dragged by its four-wheel drive and the good front tires. The clip emptied, and Bolan pulled the AutoMag as the jeep spun into the trees.

Getting to his feet, Bolan started after it when something caught his eyes against the green. Stark white, it hovered like a ghost just beyond the clearing, hovering among the trees. Bolan raced toward it, letting the image sharpen in his vision like a growing crystal. He already knew what it was, but he plunged on.

Bolan drew to within ten feet when he stopped. He couldn't come any closer. He dropped to his knees. The ap-

parition, all too real now, floated above him. Five feet off
the ground.

A rough board had been fixed to a tree at right angles.
And there, on the makeshift cross, hung the body of a man,
his hands pinned to the board by a pair of survival knives.
His ankles and arms were bound to the wood with thick
wire, one foot almost severed. Someone had crucified him,
then used him for target practice. A glitter in the bright sun
caught Bolan's eye. It took him a moment to realize what
had been tugging so anxiously at his attention. It was the
knife through the man's heart, its ivory inlay made even
whiter by the sun.

There, like all would-be messiahs before him, his clothing scarlet and sagging with the weight of blood, hung
Thomas Colgan.

21

They found the compound a little before sundown. Bolan left Carlos and Marisa in the jeep to take a closer look. After the primitive ruins of the NPA camp, the headquarters of the Leyte Brigade looked like a Pentagon prize-winning design.

From a hundred yards away, Bolan could see the floodlights glinting on the lavish coils of razor wire. As the night chill moved in, a slight breeze fluttered reluctantly and the tight coils trembled. Shimmering under the harsh halogen glare, they looked as if they were spun of light itself by some mysterious spider.

Bolan pushed deep into the trees to make a wide recon circuit. He placed every step as carefully as a choreographer. He knew Harding by type, and the high-tech wizardry of modern warfare brought a thankful tear to every Charles Harding's eye. What a joy it was to see science, for once, in the service of something useful. That was the mentality, and the Charles Hardings of the world were all the same in their chidlike fascination.

Using a small light and shielding it with his palm, Bolan quickly found the first strip of sensing wire half-buried in the leaves. He was pleased to have found it, and worried, too. Where there was one, there were bound to be others. Looking carefully, he quickly spotted four more, strung at odd distances one from another to pick up any stride, regardless of its length.

For a moment he wondered whether they might even have seismic sensors. It was a distinct possibility, but there was just so much caution even a paranoid could take. Bolan was anything but paranoid, but he wasn't reckless, either. He was a man who knew his abilities and, more importantly, their limits. Once past the pressure net, he would have to take his chances.

He still used the light, worried more now about trip wires than detection gear. If they knew he was there, that was one thing. If he triggered a claymore and blew himself to hell, that was another matter. Seen once, it was something you didn't forget. Ever. And he'd seen it more times than he could count.

In tight, the razor wire stopped shimmering. It lost its neutral beauty and he could see it for the ugly stuff it was. He didn't have anything to cut it, and it was more than likely wired, in any case. There would be no surreptitious entry by simply climbing over the fence. That was clear enough. If he was going to get in, he was going to have to work at it. While he debated what to do, the floods went out, and Bolan heaved a deep sigh of relief. Something was going his way at last.

After the circuit he dropped back to consider his options. The camp itself nagged him. It struck a resonant chord, but it took him a while to place it. Something about the layout seemed familiar. Using the light, he did a quick sketch. As he scratched the last couple of buildings in place, it hit him: it was the same as Colgan's camp.

At first blush, that made no sense until the common link jumped out and bit him—McRae. The bastard must have laid them both out. He must have been in Harding's pocket for a long time, maybe from the very beginning. Hell, he might even have done a little judicious prodding here and there, steering the hapless do-gooder without Colgan even realizing it. That would be typical of outsize egos. They had a tendency to follow while thinking they were leading. And

they usually ended up just like Colgan. Che did it, and so
did Lumumba. It was the fashionable thing. And every single nearsighted fool told himself the same thing—it won't
happen to me, brother.

Bolan couldn't be sure, but he'd seen no evidence the razor coils had been electrified. If they weren't plugged in, and
it looked like he'd have to chance it, he just might be able to
go up and over. The fence itself was sturdy cyclone web. The
posts had been anchored in concrete, the bottom of the cyclone itself trenched and cemented. There would be no going
under, not without a half-dozen hard hats and a backhoe.
That meant up and over, while avoiding wire as voracious
as a hungry shark.

He had seen some bamboo that looked fairly sturdy.
Dropping back away from the fence, he searched it out.
Appraising it with the small torch, he shook his head un-
certainly. As he hacked away at the most likely looking
trunk, he found it hard to believe bamboo was in the grass
family. The serrated edge of the survival knife scraped and
scratched on the tough fiber, but eventually cut all the way
through.

It had taken considerable effort to cut the one piece, and
that meant a ladder was out of the question. He didn't have
time. Fallback was an Olympic nightmare. But when you
had to pole vault, you ran like hell and hoped your behind
didn't end up like a stack of cold cuts somewhere in the
middle of the shiny wire.

A single light burned in one of the huts, and Bolan paced
while he waited for it to go out. He checked his watch and
set the timer. Ten minutes—that was all he was prepared to
wait. Then, come hell or high wire, he was going up and
over. He knew that kind of setup well enough to know that
most of the men were already asleep. The few who were
awake were probably lying on their cots, staring at the dark
ceiling, wondering why they had come to such a godfor-
saken hellhole in the first place. They ticked off the credits,

subtracted the debits and wondered just how close they were to breaking even.

He looked at his watch, and the timer read ten minutes while the seconds and tenths whizzed on like cars on a freeway.

It was time.

The approach wasn't that long, but the fence wasn't that high, and he wouldn't be setting a world record. He measured the run and cleared a spot to plant the hole. He had only one chance, and it had better work. Tamping the damp earth to solidify it, he tried the short sprint without the pole. When he was convinced he had a shot, he tossed the M-16 over the fence, then slipped the magazines through the wire. Making sure the AutoMag and Beretta were secure, he hefted the pole, then took a deep breath.

His first approach was all wrong, and he stopped just short of slamming into the fence. Bolan backed up for another go. On the next try, he altered his stride just enough, planted the sturdy bamboo and hurled himself toward the sky. The bamboo wasn't as flexible as he would have liked, and his shoulder sockets felt as if they'd been filled with hot lead, but the pole held and he clung fast. As he sailed over the wire, he closed his eyes and braced himself for the impact.

Bolan landed heavily. He lay there, listening to the bamboo still rattling the wire while he caught his breath. He got to his knees, rubbing his left shoulder. It burned a little, but the arm moved, and he shrugged off the pain. Gathering his ammunition and the rifle, he moved along the fence until he was right behind the middle building. If he was right about McRae, this would house the arsenal.

It was the only windowless building, and the front door was locked. He realized there was something to be said for arrogance—as long as it was the enemy's—as he slipped around to the front door. Relying on technology instead of humanity, Harding—or whoever passed for a honcho at the moment—had chosen not to post sentries. That was his second big plus, and Bolan was not unappreciative.

Keeping his ears open, he used the survival knife to carve through the wood around the padlocked latch. It took several tries, but he managed to loosen the lag bolts enough to pry the latch free. Inside he closed the door with relief. For a few minutes he'd be safe from discovery. Using the small light again, he took inventory of the large room. Just as he'd suspected, it contained nothing but munitions. But how was he to take on an unknown number of men, even if he had control of their backup firepower?

A crate of LAW rockets was part of the answer, but only part. He pulled the crate over near the door. An M-60 was another part, if he could find the ammo. It took a few minutes. The quartermaster was anything but systematic. The stuff was piled haphazardly, without regard to any rational order he could discover. The search paid off, though, in something better: a spare M-134 Minigun for one of the choppers, a folding mount already attached. It sat in a dolly with a 3000-round canister. He didn't need the M-60 now, or its ammo. His first inclination was to blow the arsenal first, but he might need something when this was all over. The LAWs were eleven pounds apiece, and the crate weighed a ton. He pried it open and removed six of the drab-looking tubes.

Bolan worked quickly, wanting to do as much as he could inside. Once the fireworks started, there would be no time for second thoughts and should haves. He got a dozen LAWs fire-ready, then checked the magazine of the minigun. It was loaded for more than bear, chock full of 7.62 mm killers.

Bolan opened the door and jammed a sliver of crating under it to keep it open. He sprinted straight across the compound, over near the gate, and stacked an armful of LAWs. A second trip put the rest of the dozen in place.

One more turn, this time waddling under the dolly weight of the minigun, and he was ready, except for the lights. He couldn't leave them intact. He had little enough edge as it was. If he sat there under the sudden siege of illumination, he'd be a sitting duck. As it was, after the first startling seconds of his onslaught, somebody was bound to figure out where he was. The LAWs would give him away, or the flashes from the Minigun. But at least he'd be a shadow in a sea of other shadows, no more substantial than a wave in an ocean full of them. And no less elusive.

Grabbing his rifle, Bolan moved quickly to the mess hut, following the fence. If he was right about the layout, that's where the main power supply was. The generator was the key. Disable it, and he would have the night and its friendly darkness as an ally. At the back of the mess hut, he pried the screen loose and crawled in through the open window.

In a corner of the modified field kitchen, the generator sat like a hulking dinosaur crouched on stubby legs. He played the flashlight across its surface until he found the main cable. Socketed and screwed in, it was just a simple matter to unscrew the sleeve and pull the plug. Just to be sure, he slashed at the cable and severed the end. They could pull all the switches and throw all the levers they wanted. With the main cable down, the camp would stay black.

After slipping back out the window, Bolan retraced his steps along the fence. One final adjustment occurred to him. He strung the LAWs along the fence, about ten feet apart. Now he could fire one and move. Let them scorch the air behind him all they wanted—he'd be long gone.

For a second he thought about Marisa and Carlos, sitting there in the dark. He wondered what they would think at the first explosion. There was no way he could have told them, because he hadn't known what he was going to do, and the time for warning them was long past.

It was time to go to work.

22

The first rocket left the tube with a throaty growl. It streaked across the compound, a thin stream of smoke trailing behind it, and slammed into the nearest hut. Dead on target, it punched through a screen and crashed out a window. A single mushrooming flame speared up through the ruptured roof. Pieces of the tarpaper sheating and long slivers of wood cartwheeled through the air, starkly outlined by the brilliant yellow flash. A fraction of a second later the baritone crump of the detonation rolled across the yard.

Gouts of flame spouted up through the broken roof. By the time the ball of smoke gave way to a slender column, Bolan was already on the move.

The second rocket went off with the same result, and added its lights to the growing illumination. The first shouts started, little more than confused bellowing, as the third LAW found its target. Bolan chucked the empty and useless tube away and moved to the fourth.

Zeroing in through the bluntly utilitarian sight, he saw a door fly open two huts down from his target and shifted his aim. The rocket homed in and knocked a string bean of a man off his feet as it grazed him before entering through the open doorway. It took out the back wall, and the slender man, wearing nothing but khaki shorts, spun out through the door, carried along by the force of the explosion.

In quick succession, Bolan let fly with three more before the first sporadic fire cracked. None of the slugs came near him, and even the noise of the gunfire seemed tame under the deepening roar of the burning buildings. As nearly as he could tell, the men still had no idea of Bolan's firing location.

Stunned by the suddenness of the attack and the terrible destruction already inflicted, the surviving members of the Leyte Brigade started to stretch a ragged blanket of fire across the compound.

Several of them sprinted into the shadows between the undamaged huts. They would be coming for him, Bolan knew, but there was still time to take out the rest of the buildings.

Staying close to the ground, he rolled from rocket launcher to rocket launcher. Bolan took out two more buildings, catching the supply shed as well as another barrack hut. Secondary explosions, probably gasoline or kerosene, tore the supply dump to pieces as easily as if it had been made of cheap cardboard. Great slabs of the wall pinwheeled away from the huge balloon of liquid flame and tumbled to the ground. It looked as if a house of cards had been set on fire. The flammable liquid in drums kept exploding, and every blast spewed scorching flame, spreading the blaze and setting fire to the hut on either side.

Bolan let his last LAW loose and crawled to the Minigun on its tripod. He scanned the dancing flames, holding fire until he had something real to shoot at. The flames twitched and twisted, tossing strange, gnarled shadows at one another, letting some fall on the ground and ooze out toward him as the flames grew taller.

At the far end of the compound, he spotted something, but the distorted light wouldn't let him focus on it long enough to make out what it was. A second later a spray of fire whistled across the compound toward him. It happened in a split second, but he could see it so clearly and his instincts were so perfectly attuned that he rolled away from the long, jagged burst even before he realized it had been fired.

Someone in the darkness had seen him, and that someone had a machine gun, an M-60 from the sound of it. Only four buildings remained intact. He had left the arsenal by design, and there had been no need to take out the mess hut. The remaining two looked almost transparent. The roaring holocaust heated the air and it surged and swelled like a translucent curtain. Things shimmered as if they were sculpted of Jell-O instead of wood and metal. The men who dashed back and forth behind the wall of flame themselves looked as if they had melted, strangely curled and fluid, like candles left out in the sun.

Bolan rolled back to the Minigun and swung it toward the knot of men against the far fence. He couldn't see them, but he knew they were there. The fire from the far end had stopped, and Bolan opened up with the Mini.

He played it across the compound, chewing at the wreckage and ripping everything in its path to pieces. Hunks of burning lumber flew into the air. Charred timbers suddenly exploded in showers of sparks, then toppled over.

Short bursts of return fire, mostly from automatic rifles and a couple of handguns, started to chip away at the ground on either side. The fence behind him rattled, and he heard several wires sing as they parted like snapped piano strings. They were getting the range, and he couldn't see them.

The Mini was almost as much a liability as an asset. It was too awkward to move, and he sure as hell wasn't going to try to carry it in some headlong charge across the open ground. He ripped one more sustained burst across the flames, letting off the trigger only long enough to spare the arsenal, then dodged away from the gate into the diminishing dark.

Along the fence, the flames still cast little more than stray patches of orange light, and Bolan was following it when a slab of shadow suddenly detached itself from the night and screamed toward him. It took a second to realize it was a jeep. The steady fire from a rear-mounted M-60 sieved through the fence right behind him as he ran, then arced its way off into the jungle night.

Swinging the M-16 around, he held it in his left hand and fired back as he ran. The chattering of the M-60 grew intermittent, as if the gunner couldn't keep his hand steady and his finger on the trigger. The jeep's headlights speared out at him all of a sudden. He felt for a moment like a butterfly pinned on a mat.

Bolan spun about and dropped to one knee. With the M-16 on his hip, he sliced across the front of the charging jeep. Both headlamps blew, each pulsing once briefly and brightly, then dying in a shower of glass and sparking filament. The jeep's radiator had been punctured, and watery steams geysered through a dozen holes. A small cloud ballooned up around the hood, but the jeep kept coming.

Bolan raised his sights for another slice, this time just over the hood, and the windshield went in a shower of glass slivers. He saw the machinegunner reach for his throat as he tumbled back over the tail and disappeared. The jeep started to weave, and Bolan realized he hadn't seen a driver.

A big front tire narrowly missed him as he dove to one side. Turning as the jeep rushed by, he caught a glimpse of the driver, crouched down behind the wheel, steering by feel and memory. The face looked oddly familiar, but it was in profile and half-hidden by steam.

The driver straightened up for a moment, wrestling with the wheel. The jeep slewed to the left, narrowly avoiding the fence. Bolan whipped his rifle in a tight arc. It burped a half-dozen rounds before the magazine ran out. The left rear tire blew, and the jeep zigzagged as the driver desperately fought the drag.

Getting to his knees, Bolan rammed a new clip home as the driver leapt from the jeep, letting it career on its own.

Bolan brought his own weapon to bear and squeezed. A single shot cracked from the M-16, then the rifle went suddenly dumb in his hands. It had jammed. He reached for the release, but the charging driver opened up. The big guy hit the deck, rolling toward the fence as he struggled to yank the AutoMag free of its holster.

The big .44-caliber automatic was slippery in his sweat-drenched hands, but he managed a single shot, forcing his opponent to dive. The unchauffeured jeep slammed into the fence, its momentum carrying it partway up the wire before it tipped over on its side, tires spinning uselessly.

Somewhere behind him, Bolan heard two sharp bursts of fire. They sang past his ear and slammed into the jeep. The fuel tank ruptured, and Bolan pressed himself flat as he saw the first spark hit a stream of gasoline. It caught and licked back up until the tank blew with a thunderous roar.

The driver lost his balance and his weapon at the same time, and Bolan charged, hitting him dead center with a vicious cross-body block. The man fell backward, and Bolan pinned him to the ground, planting a knee on each of his arms.

A slug from somewhere in the dark caught him high on the shoulder, knocking him to the ground as the driver twisted free. Scrambling around on all fours, he was looking for his rifle. Running feet thudded heavily on the ground, and Bolan turned toward the sound. Four of them, all armed with automatic rifles, charged across the compound in a tight knot.

Bolan's fist closed over the AutoMag as a light speared out of the night from beyond the fence. With a sudden roar, a jeep thundered toward the compound gate. It hit dead center and kept on coming. The four charging mercs froze in their tracks. They watched the assault of the jeep as if paralyzed.

The dual gates bulged in the middle as the driver floored it. In slow motion, the fence seemd to crumple as the gates reached their limit. The double chain snapped with a sound like pistol shots, and the roaring jeep tossed the double gates aside.

The mercs, as if controlled by a single brain, swung their rifles around to ace the new challenge. It all seemed to happen in slow motion, and the tableau seemed frozen for a moment. Bolan could see it all clearly etched against the wall of orange light chewing at the ruined camp.

Backlit by the holocaust, the mercs had been reduced to black silhouettes. The only one moving was the driver of the jeep. As Carlos jumped down, rifle in hand, time cracked open again, and things moved furiously, as if to make up for lost time and get the universe back on track.

The mercs moved as Carlos leapt. The other driver, also released from his paralysis, scooped his rifle off the ground. Carlos opened up, sweeping a viscious figure 8 through the knot of mercs. They scattered, but Bolan couldn't tell whether they'd been hit or chosen to dive out of the line of fire.

Charging ahead, his wounded arm flapping uselessly at his side, Bolan barreled into the other driver, knocking him backward again and sending his rifle cartwheeling away. Bolan lost his grip on the AutoMag, and the driver landed a sharp jab on the gunshot wound. A flash of bright light momentarily blinded Bolan as the arm went numb and he dropped to his knees.

The driver regained his footing and charged, knocking Bolan onto his back and pinning him. Bolan reached out with his one good arm, but the driver slapped it aside and locked his fingers around Bolan's throat. The flames climbed higher, and the driver turned. For the first time, Bolan recognized Don McRae.

He pushed with all his weight, closing off Bolan's air. The light began to fade, and Bolan felt tired. He realized he was on the verge of blacking out, but all the strength seemed to have been drained from his body. He was aware of the pressure on his throat and of McRae's grinning face. His fingers clawed at the man's hands, but he was ineffective.

Over and over, McRae's lips moved, but Bolan heard nothing but a ringing in his ears. Then he realized that McRae was shouting, "Die, you bastard!" With every shout, he slammed his weight forward a little harder.

Galvanized by the demanding need to do something, Bolan groped for the Beretta. His fingers closed over a handle, and he pulled it free. It felt unfamiliar, and hazily Bolan realized it wasn't the Beretta as he brought it up and shoved with his last ounce of energy. It slipped between bones all the way to the hilt, and McRae twitched. His hands seemed to be the first to realize he'd been hurt, and they relaxed their grip. His arms were still rigid for a moment, then they, too, went slack, and Bolan choked down lungfuls of air.

McRae fell to his side with a great moaning sigh. Bolan tried to pull himself free, but he didn't have the strength. Vaguely aware of McRae's weight still pressing down on him, he watched from a great distance as the world began to spin. The orange light danced on the handle of the knife, the flames glittering on the pure-white ivory inlay. Bolan thought it somehow fitting that McRae should be gravely wounded with his own knife, the same knife he'd used to torture the captives and to kill Thomas Colgan.

Then the world turned into a dark swirl, and he felt hands tugging at him just before he blacked out.

23

Bolan eased out of the car and let the door close softly behind him. The alley was pitch-black, and the air was thick with humidity and rich Chinese spices. Ongpin at night was like a piece of China moved two thousand miles and grafted on to a tropical island. As they had every place they'd settled, the Chinese had chosen to isolate themselves, keeping their culture intact, along with its wariness of foreigners.

Ongpin reflected that isolation, but unlike the last time Bolan had visited, the quarter seemed alive. Noise drifted through the open windows and the bright cracks under every door. As he moved down the alley, Bolan heard the melancholy wail of a *biwa*, its plaintive tune sounding surprisingly like the blues.

Mingling with the music, a different kind of sound drifted into the alley—voices in urgent conversation. Bolan glided cautiously, keeping to the wall. He had three more blocks to go, slipping along back fences silently, his ears alert for every jarring note. Somewhere ahead, in a nondescript building, Charles Harding and Juan Rizal Cordero polished their plans to unleash a terror on Manila the likes of which it had never known.

Looking back on it, trying to piece it all together, Bolan realized that he had been a blind man in the desert. Walt Wilson had known more than he'd revealed, but not much. Frank Henson, his hooks only barely into Colgan, had a lead, but that must have been Harding's doing. It had been a way to keep tabs on Bolan. And with McRae on the scene, it was as good as having a beeper on him.

Harding had stayed offstage, disappearing into the darkness of the wings as surely as the Phantom of the Opera. He had come and gone, leaving nothing behind but blood and ragged bits of flesh. And for what? To control a country that hadn't been up off its knees in three hundred years. Harding had been obsessed, and he had exploited others who were similarly obsessed though less clever. Men like McRae, who didn't care about anything as long as the pay was good, he bought.

Bolan wanted to get Harding like he hadn't wanted anyone in a long, long time. Seeing a city at night, spread out under the stars as defenseless as a sleeping child, vulnerable as a naked woman, really brings it home just how easy it is to make it wake up screaming.

That was the key to understanding men like Harding and Cordero. They knew how easy it was. They knew, and they loved it. And Mack Bolan loved the idea of taking them down, disassembing them as totally as a child takes apart a house of blocks.

But first he had to find them. There had been enough life left in Don McRae to make him want to trade information for keeping it, but he hadn't been sure where they were hiding. He knew three addresses, and his wallet had yielded a fourth. Manila was a rabbit warren, a system of tunnels in plain sight. Under a dictator, people learn how to live two lives, to build a city within a city. Under Ferdinand Marcos, the people of the Philippines had done it, and under Corazon Aquino they had seen no reason to tear it down.

The three blocks passed in waves of light and dark, sounds swelling and fading away like waves drifting under a pier. And the first address lay before him. A ramshackle building, three stories of ordinary stone, every window dark, lay beyond a wooden palisade more ornamental than defensive in function.

Bolan scaled the fence easily, then moved close to the building through a neat garden of well-maintained shrubbery. A half flight of wooden stairs led to the back door. Bolan took the steps carefully, alert for the least indication that someone knew he was there. With his ear to the door, he strained but heard nothing.

A second-story window, the only one without bars, lay just out of reach to the left of the stairway. He had to know whether anyone hid inside, but he couldn't get in through the door without calling attention to himself. The buildings lay in an unbroken row marching off in either direction, and Bolan backed down the stairs. Over the fence, he moved three doors down to a small shop, it's back wall slashed by rickety wooden stairs. He made it over a rusty wire fence and onto the stairs, then held his breath when someone stirred inside an open window.

Soundlessly he took the next flight and crawled over the wooden parapet. Moving back the way he'd come, over the rooftops, he found a skylight in the center of Harding's building. The skylight was locked, but he could slip the lock aside by shoving a knife blade down at an angle. It slid through the rubber molding, but he had to rap the knife handle sharply with the heel of his hand before the latch clicked open.

The skylight came free with a squeak. Inside, it was as dark as the bottom of a well, and Bolan leaned in, squeezing his eyes shut to accustom them to the darkness. When he opened them again, he could see blocks of shade, but there was no way to tell whether any of them were substantial enough to hold his weight. With a shrug, he grabbed hold of the skylight ledge and dropped down, wincing as the pain shot through his wounded arm. He almost let go for a second, but bit his lip until the pain passed.

After he stilled to ready himself, he let go with both hands and landed lightly on the balls of his feet. Groping through the dark, he found a wall. Following it to the right, he bumped his knee on something, then found the molding of a door frame. He pressed an ear to the door for a moment, but whatever lay beyond was silent.

He found the knob and tested it. It rattled once, then turned easily. Gently he pulled the door toward him. The darkness was so thick that he couldn't gauge what size area lay behind the door, and he felt as though he were in a cocoon, his senses smothered by layers of cotton wool.

Bolan stopped again to listen. His own breathing echoed distantly in his ears, but he heard no other sound. It was an impossible situation. He'd have to risk using a light. The chance that it would be spotted was no greater than the risk that he'd be heard when he stumbled over a piece of furniture or kicked a wastebasket. He reached into his pocket for the flashlight, then pulled his Desert Eagle. Pointing both in the same direction, the weapon in his good hand and the flashlight in the other, he thumbed the light on. It seemed blinding after the utter blackness, and he blinked away the glare for a few seconds.

The room was a simple bedroom, the neatly made bed and a nightstand the only furniture. He moved back and trained the light into the room he'd just come from. It appeared to be a small office, one wall full of bookshelves, the other occupied by a wooden desk with a corkboard pinned to the wall just above it. Like the bedroom, it was plain and utilitarian.

He turned back and crossed the bedroom to another door. With his hand on the doorknob, he switched off the light and listened to the darkness one more time. Opening the door, he held his breath before clicking the light back on. This time he found himself staring down a narrow hallway. The plain wooden floor was clean but needed waxing. Its surface was dull, even scarred in a few places from heavy traffic over a long period of time.

He stepped into the hall, pulling the door closed but not latching it. He was almost at one end of the hall. At the op-

osite end, a stairwell led to the floor below. He moved
ghtly toward it, squeezing the butt of the Desert Eagle in
is left hand. He could feel the texture of the grip against his
alm, a strange kind of comfort.

Bolan made his way carefully down the stairs, pausing
very few steps to listen. The place might as well have been
tomb, for all the sound he heard. He'd seen model homes
hat had more life in them.

And with every step, he felt more and more certain that
e was bringing things to a head. Harding was within reach
ow, even if he still kept to the shadows. It was gut feeling,
ntuition. Information was the least of it. Bolan had a kind
f sixth sense, a radar, that never failed him.

In the dark he could hear the steady beep, beep, beep as
he beam swept past a target. The little green blip swelled
nd died, swelled and died, a light on a dim screen that cor-
esponded exactly to something real and substantial. Hard-
ng was that little green light now, and Bolan was closing in.

The next floor was as vacant as the first.

But the little light kept flashing.

24

Mack Bolan opened the heavy door, not expecting to find anything of interest but hoping he was wrong. He had gone over the first three floors, working his way down from the top. He felt like a novice cat burglar on a milk run. His technique was perfect, his haul nonexistent. With every empty room, his frustration had grown sharper. He'd had precious little time to begin with, and now he couldn't help hearing every second click away, its sharp snap echoing and fading, only to be replaced by the next one, and the next.

So far, he hadn't found a single thing to connect this place with Charles Harding, nothing except the address muscled out of a frightened man who had nothing to lose whether he lied or told the truth. And when lying might let you suck air for another thirty hours, why not do it? For that matter, Bolan still hadn't seen anything to connect this dark, empty collection of echoes with a single living soul. It was so neat and so clean that it was almost perfect.

And that was what kept him going. Such perfection just didn't exist. No one used three stories of living space without leaving a single sheet of paper out of place, a wrinkle or two on a bedspread, a dirty glass in a sink. It was almost as if someone had scurried ahead of him in the darkness, room by room, with a dust cloth in one hand and a dump sponge in the other. He doubted if a forensic team would be able to pull a single fingerprint.

And that could mean one of only two things. Either the place was supposed to look like that, in which case it was a dummy, some sort of antiseptic front meant to be seen but not used. Or it was used to hide something, and the pristine upper floors were meant simply to discourage the curious, suggesting a wrong turn had been made somewhere back three or four steps. But then the whole operation had been one long wrong turn. Nobody could flit back and forth across the Pacific like some sort of long-distance moth and vanish as completely as Charles Harding had done. Nobody, that is, except a man whose business was not meant to endure sunlight and fresh air.

As the doorknob turned, Bolan held his breath. The tension was almost palpable, and he had to fight against carelessness. How many empty rooms do you have to look into before you expect them all to be that way? Or was that what Harding was counting on?

Bolan groped inside the dark stairwell for a light switch. Neither wall had one. He clicked on his flashlight and played it over the ceiling, looking for a pullchain. The ceiling was flat and empty, and the light showed nothing on either wall. Bolan found the first step, then clicked off the flashlight as he stepped on through the door.

Feeling his way slowly down the stairs, he kept one hand on the wall to keep his balance in the dark. He nearly stumbled when he reached for another step and found himself already on a flat surface, either a floor or a landing.

One more time he'd have to risk the light. When it lanced out, the darkness seemed to swallow the beam whole. It petered out before finding anything across the floor. He swung it close and played the beam up and down the wall beside him. As it moved away, the perfect circle flattened into an oval, then an open-ended parabola. The wall was completely blank. Cinder blocks, neatly mortared and painted over with a thick, off-white gloss, stretched a good forty feet before the beam played out.

Before moving, Bolan tried to reconstruct his passage down. As near as he could figure, he was looking toward the street in front of the building, but from below street level a good ten or twelve feet, possibly even more. Bolan started along the wall, again clicking off the light and feeling his way with a cautious prodding of one foot then dragging the other up alongside it.

He was starting to feel a damp chill that had nothing to do with climate. About twenty-five feet along the wall, his foot struck something. It sounded hollow, and was probably made of wood. Bolan tried to move around it, but it was too wide for him to maintain contact with the wall. He didn't want to lose the orientation.

The light clicked on again, and seemed dimmer. The light looked pale, almost washed out, and had an orange cast. The batteries were giving out. Hurriedly he played the beam along the wall and moved around the obstacle, then clicked it off to conserve the power. He made it all the way this time without interruption. His foot struck something solid, then he leaned forward with one hand. Even in the dark he could tell it was a corner. The flat, unyielding thing in front of him was another wall, made of the same cinder block and painted with the same smooth paint.

Bolan flicked the light on one more time. He shone it on the wall in front of him, then started working it toward the left. A metallic click from somewhere off to the left jerked his head around. Instinctively he shut off the light as he dropped to the cold stone floor.

A small spurt of light flashed, and the slug slammed into the wall just over his crouching body. He heard the bullet puncture the cinder block and slap like a wet snail against the far side, then rattle down through the hollow blocks for a split second.

A second flash, almost like a powerful firefly, spat at him, and another slug cracked against the brittle blocks above him. Bolan started to roll, trying not to lose his fix on the ource of the flame. Using the light was suicide, but he ouldn't afford to let the gunman get away.

Bolan stopped rolling as he hit the wooden box he'd had o step around. Getting to his knees, he craned his head orward, turning it slightly to try and get some sense of his urroundings. In the darkness he heard something, a soft vhisk like someone sweeping a sidewalk two blocks away.

But the sound was a hell of a lot closer. As he listened, it lrew still closer, as if the gunman knew where he was. He ulled the Desert Eagle and waved the gun back and forth, rying to decide where to fire and when. Listening intently, e heard one more rasp of something on stone, then the loise stopped.

Far across the cellar, a wedge of light shone for a second, nd someone shouted. The light vanished, and a hollow oom rolled across the dark floor. A door had opened for he briefest instant, then been slammed shut. He'd seen it mmediately and felt certain that no one had slipped hrough. A man would have to be thin as a sheet of paper to nanage an entry through that narrow opening.

The shout had come from the gunman, he guessed. But n the renewed darkness, he was no better off than he had een before the door opened. Groping his way past the vooden crate, he kept low and moved as quickly as he :ould. Something smacked into his right arm, just below the vound, and he groaned involuntarily.

Two quick shots cracked, and he didn't even see any light. 3oth bullets thudded into the wooden crate, which was just a foot or two behind him. It had been close, and he knew he vas lucky the gunman was content to fire single shots. A purt of automatic fire would probably find him. The gunnan was good. He hadn't missed by much with any of the 'our shots.

Bolan realized his opponent had some unexplained advantage, and as that fact sank in, the cellar seemed to shrink around him, propelling him even closer to the gunman. The

gun barked again, and the report was louder, as if the gun
man had drawn closer. Bolan fired twice. One shot pinged
off something metal, striking it obliquely then slapping into
a solid obstacle far across the chamber. The second seemed
to disappear without a trace. No sound of bullet on un
yielding wood, stone or metal, no groan from wounded
flesh, drifted back to him. It was as if the darkness had
swallowed the bullet completely.

Bolan thought about that for a few seconds, and came to
the only conclusion possible. Somewhere almost dead ahead
of him, the chamber was open. Perhaps the room nar
rowed into a tunnel, like the one Marisa had taken him
through, or maybe an open door let the bullet pass through
and find something soft beyond it.

He started to back up, the Desert Eagle in his left hand,
his nearly useless right stroking the cold wall. Quickly, he
backtracked, stopping only when his butt slammed into the
right-angled wall. He knew the stairwell was just to his left,
and started inching toward it. As his right hand brushed
against the free wall of the stairwell, he groped gingerly with
his foot. A misstep might get him killed or, at the very least,
alert the gunman to his whereabouts.

As the sole of his boot found the rough stone of the bot
tom step, all his care was rendered pointless. The cellar
flooded with light. He dove straight ahead, just ahead of a
hail of gunfire. As he started up the stairs, he tripped and
fell. It saved his life.

A flurry of shots, this time not from any handgun,
punched through the hollow cinder blocks, scattering frag
ments all over the stairs and raining sharp chips and dust
down over his head and shoulders.

Bolan turned, lying on the stairs stiff as a board, his spine
straddling three steps. He swung the Desert Eagle around in
a two-handed grip and waited, breathing shallowly and ig
noring the hard stone digging at his backbone. He heard

them coming, their feet slapping the stone floor as they raced toward the stairs.

He didn't have to wait long. Two men, running flat out, jostled one another as they turned the corner and Bolan fired four shots. The Desert Eagle spat ferociously, and the lead man threw up his hands. His weapon, an AK-47, started up, then dropped straight down as it slipped from his grip. He fell backward, a brand new and very ugly hole just over his left eye. The remaining three shots had taken the second man in the right shoulder and in the throat. He, too, lost his weapon as his hand flew up to his neck and closed around the most serious wound. He only had strength for making a horrible rattling sound in his throat.

The lead man, who appeared to be Chinese, was considerably shorter than his companion, and his collapsing body slammed into his partner's knees. The runner-up, a skinny Anglo built like a stork, all gawky limbs and sharp features, smacked his head on the wall behind as he fell with the weight of the Chinese added to his own. A sharp crack echoed up the stairwell as he hit, and his head sat at a funny angle as he slid the rest of the way to the floor. If the bullets hadn't killed him, the broken neck would have.

Bolan scrambled back a step or two, still lying on the stairs and bumping his vertebrae against the lip of the step as he pushed with his heels. It was suddenly silent in the cellar, and Bolan panted short, sharp breaths. In the confined stairwell, they sounded like sandpaper on soft stone.

He slowly gathered his legs under him before rising. He took one step down, then another. It remained quiet, but the man with the silenced pistol hadn't been accounted for. The two men lying in an obscene heap in front of him both had automatic rifles.

Bending down, he tugged the AK up by its muzzle, then grabbed the handgrip and picked it up. He made sure it was operable, and that the magazine was at least partially loaded. Muffling the click of the reinserted magazine, he leapt to the cellar floor and swept the muzzle of the AK in a semicircle, his finger on the trigger.

A man had been caught in the hail of 7.62 mm slugs. He looked at the rip in his stomach with surprise. His right hand dropped an ugly-looking Makarov, hung in the air for a moment, then fluttered toward the dark red stains across his blue cotton shirt. He glanced at Bolan as he fell back and slammed hard into the floor.

He opened his mouth, but nothing came out. Behind him, across the stone floor, a door yawned darkly. It was the same one that had ben cracked open briefly. Bolan jerked the magazine from the second AK and started toward the open door.

As he drew close, he realized that yet another door was ajar at the far end of the chamber. It must have been the spot that had swallowed the missing shot. He would have to check it out, but first things first. Poking into the first door, he swept a palm along the wall. A fluorescent light pinged and flashed on. At first Bolan thought it was nothing more than a simple office.

Then he saw the map.

25

Bolan stared at the map for a long moment, leaning closer and reaching out to touch it. Small red circles peppered the center of Manila. A quick count showed thirty-three. All but five had been crosshatched by a makeshift star or crude asterisk. None of the locations meant anything to Bolan, who did not have that comprehensive a knowledge of the city.

Pinned to a corkboard by a half-dozen pushpins, the map appeared to be standard issue. Nearly three feet long on each side, it was creased in several places, indicating a regular fold, almost like an American road map, but the segments were twice the size. Bolan jerked the pushpins free, one by one, then folded the map carefully. He backed out of the office and climbed the stairs to the first floor.

He dialed in a hurry, then waited for someone to pick up. The phone rang several times, and Bolan impatiently waited for Marisa to answer. Finally the receiver on the other end rattled out of its cradle.

"Bring Carlos," he said, "quickly. You know where. I'll meet you out front." Bolan slammed the phone down and moved toward the front door. It was far too late to worry about caution. He stood in the front hall, pulling a plain cloth curtain aside and tucking it behind the doorknob so he could watch the street.

It was quiet out there, almost too quiet, but he couldn't afford to worry about that, either. He killed time by combining the ammo from both AKs into one magazine, then tossed the empty into a brown metal wastebasket next to a small utility table.

His arm was beginning to throb again, and he wished he had some painkillers. He squeezed the thickly bandaged wound, trying to shut out the stabbing ache. While he waited, he considered his options. They were few and unattractive. The first image of the map kept floating into his mind's eye like a dust mote and darting away every time he tried to stare at it directly.

Without a timetable, he had to assume the worst. There was no doubt at all in his mind that the red circles were significant. If Cordero was in the picture, and Bolan was certain of that, he could guess just what that significance was. But it wasn't something he could handle by himself. Even if he, Carlos and Marisa split up, they had eleven sites each to cover. But where would they begin to look without quite knowing what to look for?

On a hunch, Bolan dashed back up to the third floor without using a light. Kneeling in front of the single window in the center of the front room, he eased the shade up a fraction of an inch, then leaned forward with his chin on the sill. Despite the darkness, the sky made a decent backdrop for the broken line of rooftops across the narrow street. The buildings lay hard up against one another, allowing a determined man to make his way the length of the block by way of the roofs.

Bolan started at the corner, twisting his neck to see the building all the way on the left. One by one, he checked each roof, letting his gaze linger a minute or so. He didn't know what he was looking for, or even if there was anything to see, but there was no point in being careless.

He'd checked the first eight buildings without noticing anything out of place. The ninth, too, was still. His eyes were adjusted to the gloom, and the slight blue cast of the sky seemed brighter behind the stark black of the shadowy buildings. The tenth was almost directly across the street, offset by half its width. Like the others, it had a low parapet extending the front wall a couple of feet above the roof. But it, too, seemed lifeless.

A bright glare off to the left distracted him, and light washed up and over the storefronts as a vehicle entered the street a block away. It was moving slowly, and he was still unable to see it when the light went out for a moment, then flashed back on. Bolan moved to the edge of the window, trying to get a fix on the vehicle, but it seemed to have stopped on the far side of the cross street. The lights went out, and a door slammed.

For three minutes he heard nothing more. He went back to scanning the roof across the street. His eyes had to readjust after the brightness of the headlights. He thought he saw something that hadn't been there before, but he wasn't sure. Blinking to wash away the lingering effect of the light, he squeezed his lids down tight and held them there for ten or fifteen seconds.

When he looked back, the thing he'd seen was gone, if it had ever been there. Checking his watch, he realized he only had ten minutes before Carlos and Marisa were due to arrive. He inspected the next building and the next, then darted his eyes back to the eleventh. Something had moved—he was certain of it.

Backing away from the window, he started to run, slowing only when he sensed the door frame. He reached for it, brushed it with a hand as he went by and clicked on the flashlight as he reached the head of the stairs. Taking the steps two at a time in the pale tangerine wash of the dying torch, he made the turn, sprinted down the second-floor hall and headed into the last just as the light died altogether.

He found the back door locked with one of those double-key affairs. Bolan moved to the nearest window and ripped the curtain aside. The window was barred, but the lock didn't look all that secure. He raised the sash, planted a foot on the widnow gate and shoved. The gate popped out of its channel, but didn't give. Pushing again, he felt it spring back and forth like a trampoline under his foot, but he wasn't getting enough leverage to force it loose.

Using his foot again, he forced the gate out far enough to slip the AK between it and the sill. Handling the Russian rifle like a crowbar, he managed to get the latch twisted out of shape, but it still wouldn't give. He couldn't use the front, and he didn't want to risk too much noise at the back.

Running back up to the ungated second-floor window, he raised the sash and swung out over the weedy garden below. Pushing off with his feet, he launched himself into a clump of shrubbery. The bushes broke his fall, and he untangled himself with just a handful of scratches. Sprinting down the back alley, he reached the corner and skidded into a turn. A dog barked in one of the buildings as he ran past.

The side street was black and empty as an abandoned mine. A single light burned far down the next block as Bolan reached the intersection. As fast as he could, he covered the open space to the far side and moved on down to the alley behind the opposing row of buildings. Two doors in, he spotted a fire escape and hurdled a small fence into another garden.

Bolan had to leap to catch hold of the metal ladder and, grimacing at the pain in his wounded arm, grabbed on and hauled himself up to the first landing. He tried to muffle the sound of his boots on the metal grating and the stairs leading to the third floor. Balancing on the railing, he could reach over the roof far enough to grab the inner side of the low brick wall and pull himself up and over.

The roof was a wilderness of pipes and little stone walls, vents wearing coolie hats and black boxes lined with glass reflecting starlight through the rain-spotted dust. Quickly Bolan approached to within two roofs of the building that had so fascinated him. He remembered his last time in this part of Manila and the shadows flitting along the roofline.

They had caught him by surprise that time, and if it hadn't been for Marisa, who knew how it would have ended. But this time the joke was on them.

As he stopped carefully over another of the diminutive walls, lights flashed into the streets below. The sound of an idling engine drifted through the night, and Bolan picked up his pace. As he ducked behind the stubby chimney, he heard the faint scuffing of feet against the sandy tar ahead of him. He knelt to peer around the roughly mortared stone. Three men, strung across the parapet on their knees, trained rifles on the street below.

The AK was the only solution.

Bolan jerked the assault rifle off his shoulder and swung the muzzle around. The sound of the approaching jeep grew louder, echoing up from the narrow street and rambling across the roof. Its headlights splashed on the tops of the buildings across the street, and Bolan found himself wondering how the assassins knew to be there, but he didn't have to wonder long. It struck him with an almost physical force, like a blow in the chest—Harding was still one step ahead of him. He must have a tap on the phone. He must have guessed that Bolan, if he escaped the ambush in the cellar, might use the phone.

But Bolan pushed the thought aside. At this point it really didn't matter how the hell they came to be there. What counted now was taking them out. The jeep in the street below stopped with a squeak of its brakes as Bolan started his move. He could see the nearest gunman tense, then lean forward a little farther. Bolan squeezed the AK's trigger and swept the muzzle in a vicious line, just about even with the top of the parapet. Any higher, and the stray slugs would rip into the buildings across the street. Any lower, and they wouldn't be lethal.

The assassin on the left gave a startled "oohh" and tried to rise, then fell backward. His gun pitched forward over the wall, and Bolan heard it slam onto the pavement below as his deadly burst stretched along the wall, chipping at the concrete slab on its top and sparking in bright showers.

The second gunman had started to turn as Bolan opened up, almost as if some instinct had heard something not yet audible. Clean as a straight razor, the AK sliced across his midsection just above the hips, and he fell over the wall.

The third man had time to turn all the way around, his own rifle clutched in one hand. He started to roll, losing his grip on the gun and leaving it behind as he tumbled across the tar. The AK gouged the tar and chewed its way toward him faster than he could roll. One hand reached up and out toward Bolan as if the man wanted to ask him for a favor.

But it was far too late for favors of any kind, and certainly for mercy. Bolan had seen too many lifeless bodies in the final insult of early and violent death. The third gunner's body twitched like a spastic puppet, his legs bouncing off the tar once or twice before he lay still.

Bolan dashed to the wall and looked down into the street. Carlos and Marisa crouched behind the jeep, Carlos sweeping his M-16 back and forth, waiting for something to shoot at while Marisa clapped her hands over her ears. Her mouth was open as if she were shouting, but he heard nothing.

In the dark street he could see little more than that and ducked away just as Carlos spotted him and snapped off a single shot. The concrete cracked, and a sliver sliced through Bolan's sleeve as he fell back out of the way. Crawling on his back for a few feet, he jumped up and sprinted back toward the fire escape.

Not worrying about the noise anymore, he landed with a thud on the top landing, then half stepped and half slid down the two flights of iron stairs. Not bothering with the ladder, he dropped into the garden and leapt back over the wall into the alley.

He reached the street in a half-dozen strides, skidded onto the pavement and raced to the corner. Shielding himself, he called out and saw Carlos turn to look toward him. He waved a hand, and Carlos brought his gun around but didn't fire. Cautiously Bolan stepped into the street. He heard Marisa whisper something, and Carlos muttered an answer before standing.

Bolan waved him to the corner and he saw Carlos tug Marisa to her feet as he rushed past and down to the back alley. Bolan waited just long enough to see Carlos wheel around the corner, Marisa right behind him. He dashed to the rear of Harding's building and leapt the fence. Carlos helped Marisa over, then took her hand again and joined Bolan on the stairs.

Bolan fired a short burst through the door, then ripped it open and pushed it aside for Carlos and Marisa. He followed them inside, leaving the door ajar. Taking the lead, he barged into the stairwell and down to the still-brightly-lit cellar.

In the small office, he pulled the map from his pocket and spread it on the desk.

"Look at this," he said.

Carlos braced himself with a hand on either side of the map and leaned forward to get a closer look.

Bolan stabbed a finger at one of the circles. "Where is this? What's there, what sort of building?"

"The train station, Señor Belasko."

"And here?"

"I'm not sure. Some stores, a concert hall, a museum."

"Here?"

"The Supreme Court is on one side of the square, the south side. On the north, some government buildings, city government, mostly..."

"Take this to Captain Roman Collazo, the Military Police building. Give it to him and tell him there could be a bomb at every one of those circles. I'm not sure which buildings, and I don't even know for sure whether they've been planted already or not. I only know that Harding has plans for those locations, and Cordero's probably been to half of them—maybe the ones that have an '*X*' on them. "Tell him I'll be in touch."

"What about Señora Colgan?"

"She's coming with me. I need her help."

"Where are you going, *señor*?"

"Underground, Carlos. I have a feeling Mr. Harding is expecting me...."

26

Marisa, you don't have to do this if you don't want to."
Bolan watched her face closely, but she betrayed no hesita-
tion.

"Of course not, but I want to."

"Are you sure?"

"Yes...I...I know what you thought of my husband, Mr.
Belasko, but I still think he was right. He stood for some-
thing. I have to see that Harding pays for that. For Thomas.
If you can make that happen..."

Bolan nodded gravely. "All right, then, let's go. You
know the tunnels. Where do you think Harding would be?
Where would he feel the most secure?"

"I can only guess."

"That's all we've got, Marisa. And we don't have time to
guess wrong."

She nodded. "I'm ready."

Bolan waited while she took a deep breath. She placed a
hand on his forearm for a moment, and he moved toward
the door. He stopped at the mouth of the tunnel and made
sure his flashlight was working. He clicked it on and trained
it into the darkness. The beam was steady and, unlike the
smaller torch, its light was clear and white.

"You'd better not use that."

She was right, so he clicked the light off, tucked it into his
pocket and stepped through the opening. Marisa squeezed
past him to take the lead.

In the darkness he could hear her fingers brushing the wall, and her steps were measured and slow, as if she were counting paces. It was so unlike his first passage through the underground, the breakneck pace even more incredible now that she moved so deliberately.

In a hoarse whisper she said, "I'm sorry to be so slow, but I'm not as familiar with this tunnel as I am with some of the others. I don't quite know where we'll end up, but if Harding came this way, we'll find him. There are just so many tunnels, just so many places he could be."

Her whisper died away, its echo drifting back from far down the tunnel like the shuffle of soft paper in small hands. Bolan felt blind in the darkness, but they couldn't run the risk of a light. It was up to Marisa, and they both knew it.

"Just do what you can," Bolan said softly. He didn't have high hopes for their success but didn't want to discourage her.

Every step seemed to take a century as they groped through the tunnel. Neither of them spoke, and Bolan found himself wondering about Marisa. In some way he couldn't quite explain, she seemed different, more like an automaton than the fiercely independent woman she had been before her husband's death. She had changed, as if part of her strength had come from him.

She seemed narrowed somehow, focused in a way he had seen before, had even sensed in himself on occasion. He recognized that part of Marisa had reduced the population of the planet to two people alone: herself and Charles Harding. To Bolan, it was a misplaced devotion to Thomas Colgan. But to Marisa, and he couldn't argue with her feelings, it was retribution mandated by a law she neither controlled nor understood. She was running on pure courage with one thought in her mind: make the bastard pay.

Bolan sensed something of that same fierce concentration in himself. He had seen the handiwork of the man and thought Charles Harding had a price to pay, exacted in the only currency that mattered. For Bolan, as for Marisa, an eye required an eye, a tooth demanded a tooth.

Cordero, of course, was part of the mix, but Bolan considered him secondary, an implement more than a man, something that Harding would use and throw away. It was the age of disposables, in everything from paper plates to hypodermics. Why should an instrument of terror be any different?

Take Harding down, and Cordero would wither, an unpicked fruit in an abandoned garden.

Take Harding down, Bolan thought—the only way to go. But first, he reminded himself, you had to find him.

"Wait a minute," Marisa whispered, her voice almost reverent, as if she were in the nave of some gloomy cathedral instead of a catacomb under a city on the brink of annihilation. "It should be here." She let go of Bolan's arm, and he heard her feet shuffle on the damp stone underfoot, the faint splash of her shoe in the shallow stream coursing through the tunnel. "It has to be here."

"What are you looking for?"

"There is supposed to be an outlet here, on the right. Let me go a little farther."

Her feet scraped on the stone again, scattering little splashing sounds as she moved. Her palm slapped against the damp stone, its sound swallowed after a single dull echo.

"Where is it?" She sounded almost petulant, as though someone had found something she had hidden and thought secure. The palm slapped harder against the stone. Her voice tightened and rose in pitch, just a notch, but Bolan caught it.

Don't lose it now, Marisa—not now, he thought.

"Maybe the light . . ."

"*No!* I don't need light. It's here or it isn't."

Bolan pulled the flashlight out of his pocket. Muffling the switch, he clicked it on and trained it on the wall. And it stared him in the face. She was right, there should have been an opening. There was, in fact a new section of wall, the mortar still bright, the surface of the stone almost free of lichens.

"Forget about it. We'll have to find some other way."

She shook her head angrily.

"What do we do now?" Bolan asked.

"We have to go out of our way, that's all."

Bolan clicked the light off again. "Lead the way," he said.

He heard Marisa move away. She no longer reached back for him; it was as though she was trying to separate herself from him, perhaps to prove something to him, or to herself. She was setting a faster pace, either because she knew they had some distance to cover or because she wanted to show that she, too, was aware of the urgency of their purpose. Bolan was glad to see that independent streak, an awareness of herself, an awareness that there was still more to her life than simple vengeance.

The bricked-up wall bothered him. It gave Harding an elusive edge. By changing the ground rules, he was taking charge of the situation. It also meant that Harding might be leading them on, funneling them to some place where that advantage would do him the most good. But that awareness did not change anything. Bolan had no choice, and Harding knew it.

It was a goading kind of challenge. It amounted to saying try to beat me with a stacked deck, big guy. I dare you.

Every step brought them closer to the last hand, and Bolan only had a single edge: he knew Harding wasn't bluffing.

Marisa had settled into a steady rhythm, and they were making good time. Bolan was relieved, at least, that the uncertainty was gone. He had been bearding the lion in his den, and the lion had finally been heard from. With that out of the way, there was simply the matter of staying alive. And

e thought of the camp, the high-tech defenses, and his
lood went cold.

"Marisa, stop!" he said urgently, then clicked on the light
nd aimed it far down the tunnel. Marisa flinched at the
udden glare, but said nothing. Bolan chewed on his lower
ip, trying to sort things out.

"I want you to stay here," he said at last.

"But you need me to guide you...."

"I'll do without."

"You're crazy!"

"Maybe. But I don't think so. I've just gotten a little in-
ight into Harding."

"What're you thinking?"

"I'm thinking Harding has set this up so there's only one
vay we can go. Because he wants us some place in particu-
ar. I'm also thinking that he's counting on our using the
larkness to cover our approach. Which means..."

"Which means he may have boobytrapped the tunnels,
ight?"

"Right. He's assuming we won't use the light. Just like at
he camp he didn't post sentries because he assumed the
lectronics were enough. He was wrong and he knows it. But
his time he's set us loose in a maze, there's only one way
ut, and that's over him. If we get that far, and he's betting
ve won't."

"How can you be sure?"

"I can't, not completely. But it's typical of his arrogance. It's the kind of thing he would do. Sit back and smile
while the rats walk right into the meat grinder."

"Only we're not rats."

"He doesn't see that difference."

"And if you're wrong?"

"Then at least you'll be able to help Carlos explain what's
going on. Disarming whatever bombs have been planted is
creating the symptom. But Harding's the disease. He has to
be cut out, like a cancer."

"And you're the surgeon, eh, Mr. Belasko?"

"In a way."

"I think you're wrong. Dead wrong."

"No arguments, Marisa. Just do what I tell you."

"Which is?"

"Turn back . . ."

"And if I say no?"

Bolan didn't answer, only looked at her steadily. Marisa swayed on her feet a moment, as if her balance had been thrown momentarily out of kilter. Then, without a word she turned and started back the way they'd come. Bolan watched her go for a minute, her left hand lightly tracing the wall, her feet splashing softly in the water.

Turning away, Bolan played the light down the tunnel until it fell away in a gloom too deep for it to plumb. The rippling water underfoot caught the light and splashed little slivers of white and silver on the wall.

He started off quickly, but using the light to good advantage. He hadn't gone more than twenty yards before he found the first booby trap. A tiny strand of nylon, almost invisible even with the light, ran across the tunnel. He tracked it up the wall to a pair of claymores barely concealed in crevices in the tunnel roof. Either one would have been enough to kill him and bury him at the same time. The pair of them would have reduced his body to ground beef then pressed the last drop of blood out of every ounce under the crushing weight of the collapsed ceiling.

Bolan nodded grimly.

Strike one, Charlie-boy, he thought.

27

The tunnel made a sharp left, and Bolan realized he was heading toward the waterfront. The character of the passage changed, and the smooth stone gave way to rough brick. Water trickled down the walls from the storm drains above him, and there was a scurrying that preceded him, always just out of reach of the flashlight.

He found the second trap about a hundred feet after the turn. Again it was a simple contrivance of nylon trip wire and a pair of claymores. He snipped the wire and left the mines in place. Disarming them was a problem for someone else.

Bolan shut off the light for a minute and paused to listen. The gurgle of running water sounded almost peaceful. But another sound, one he couldn't identify, whispered out of the darkness far ahead of him. Faint, and echoing slightly in the tight confines of the passage, it was a hum with a rough edge, as if a million bees lurked at the end of the tunnel.

He flipped the light back on and moved more swiftly. A slap behind him spun him around, and he swept the light around but could find nothing.

With a shrug he turned back and pushed on. The floor of the passage canted slightly downhill to carry the runoff from Manila's heavy tropical rains. Judging by the walls, which were relatively clean almost halfway up, but then more thickly overgrown with pale green and gray lichens, the

surge at flood must be fairly powerful. It seemed to have
scoured the lower half and kept the floor almost free of litter. Without really thinking about it, he wondered for a
moment when the rainy season started.

He almost missed the third trap. His gaze was drawn a few
paces ahead. Something about the floor that didn't look
quite right. He approached it cautiously, dropping into a
crouch and training the flashlight on a metal plate running
the width of the floor.

From ten feet away, the encrusted metal looked as if it had
been there forever. A closer look revealed a few shiny
scratches, bright metal where none should have been, that
reflected the light, winking as the half inch of water ran over
it, rippling a little as it passed over the thick lip of rusty steel.
With a combat knife, he worked the plate up, taking care
not to let it slip back. Obviously designed to respond to
pressure, the device would be harmless unless he lost his grip
and dropped the plate back into place.

It was almost six feet long and eighteen inches wide.
When it swung open, Bolan jerked it by one end, twisting
the other back away from the crevice it concealed. Training
the light into the smooth pool of water, he spotted a slab of
C-4 plastique in a clear plastic container sealed with water-
proof tape. The bomb nestled comfortably down among a
cluster of pipes that ran through the floor and disappeared
under the wall on either side. Three pressure detonators,
sprouting wires running to the plastique, were held in place
by a twist of copper wire bound to the topmost pipe.
Around each, a tight spring, resistant enough to support
only the plate, waited for a careless foot to spurt electricity
into the small detonator clearly visible through the transparent plastic. Had Bolan stepped on the plate in the dark,
he'd have been quivering jelly oozing down the wall in
nanoseconds.

Cordero's handiwork, Bolan thought.

He wondered what kind of nerve it took for a man to hunch down over that lethal package, knowing that a single mistake would blow him to pieces. But it was a peculiar courage that enabled one to take such risks, only to slaughter innocent people by the hundreds.

Carefully Bolan severed the gleaming copper holding each spring trigger in place and let all three sink into the water and out of sight. He stepped over the trench, looking back at it for a moment, then shaking his head. That one had been too close. Harding had upped the ante. I must be getting close, Bolan thought.

Bolan knew he'd been lucky that time. And he knew a man had only so much luck. He'd long since exhausted his allotment, but at the moment it was his only ally.

The tunnel started a gentle curve to the right and sloped more sharply downward. His feet started to slip on the damp stone underfoot, and he braced himself against the wall with one hand. Holding the torch in his injured hand, he tried to keep his balance without losing the slender security of the light. The floor leveled out after fifty yards or so, and he was grateful for the reprieve.

Carlos had given him his M-16, and he slipped it off his shoulder, carrying it with his finger through the trigger guard and the safety off. Every now and then the spare magazines in his pocket clicked together with a sharp snap, and he shifted one to the other side. He knew only too well that his situation was too precarious to let something like that make the difference between living and dying.

The character of the walls began to change now. In addition to the massive stonework, massive steel beams stabbed down into the ground on either side. Others, just as sturdy, bridged the paired beams. Bolan realized that the nature of the city above him had changed. Heavy weight, too heavy to rely just on stone and mortar, pressed down on the tunnel. He must have come nearly to the waterfront now, with its huge warehouses, some of them full of newly unloaded cargo and others, abandoned, lying empty and lifeless as bleached skulls on a desert floor.

He had been surprised not to have encountered an intersection, and grateful, too. Surprised because such tunnels usually snaked and interlaced in mazelike tangles, and grateful because this particular one did not. And he realized, too, that it was by design. Harding must have deliberately chosen a building giving access to a tunnel he could seal and control without attracting attention. That could only mean that Harding himself lay in wait at the end of this damp, murky passage.

Bolan shut off his light and stood still. The humming was much louder, but he still wasn't able to identify it. Turning on the light once more, he moved more quickly, watching the floor for another trap, but saw nothing. Then a heavy slam resounded through the tunnel, and shouting voices echoed off the clammy walls.

Bolan skidded to a halt and clicked off the light again. The noise intensified, as if a door had been opened somewhere on a room full of heavy machinery. Then, as suddenly as the first clap of thunder had come, the humming died, not fading away, but abruptly and completely cut off, as if something had been shut down.

A dim glow filtered to him now, but he could see nothing directly. He had to get closer, and he had to do it in the dark. Again relying on the wall to guide him, he inched forward, tensing his muscles, prepared to stop at the first sign of resistance to a poised foot. The voices continued to reverberate through the tunnel, and a spear of light slashed along the far wall from around a tight bend.

Heavy feet splashed in the water, and the light bounced up and down. Bolan flattened himself behind one of the steel pillars and pulled his Beretta out. He set it on single shot and held his breath. From the sound of things, two or three men were in the tunnel and headed his way. He eased around the pillar and skipped to the next, just before the bend in the passage. The voices sharpened, and Bolan caught a scrap of conversation as he leaned into the wall.

"Son of a bitch is probably dead. Old Juano doesn't fuck around with them traps. One of the three should have worked. Bet we find a few hunks of raw meat and a pile of rock."

"No way. We would have heard something, man."

"Not necessarily. You can't hear shit with that fucking conveyor going."

"When's it going down, anyway?"

"The witching hour, babe. In the midnight hour. Cordero blows half the city in two hours, or some shit, and then we do our thing."

They were talking about him.

And they were in for a surprise.

Bolan held the flashlight in one hand, the Beretta in the other. He aimed the flashlight along the barrel of the deadly weapon and trained both on the bend in the tunnel, his thumb poised on the light switch.

The flashlight came into view first, but Bolan waited to get a look at the odds. Behind the man with the light, in the reflected backwash, he saw two more. All three were armed with AK-47s. None of them seemed overly concerned they might not be alone in the tunnel.

Bolan aimed carefully and fired once, taking the last man out first. The Beretta spat, an ugly little cough, and the slug plowed through flesh with a wet smack and broke bone with a sharp crack. The tail stumbled, his arms just shadows flailing at his chest, then he fell over, cracking his skull against the stone wall.

His companions didn't react at first, but the man with the light seemed to have sensed something. He swiveled back and swung the light around. The second man bumped into him and nearly tripped.

"Hey, Randy. What's with you?" The man with the light seemed confused. Bolan took his companion out with his second shot. The man staggered back under the impact of the 9 mm slug. He dropped to one knee, waving his arm wildly and trying to raise his rifle to shoot something he couldn't see.

The man with the light found Randy in his beam, and Bolan saw the bright blood smeared on the shirt front.

"What the...?"

Then the light went out. Bolan heard footsteps, and he stepped away from the wall, clicking on his light at the same time. He picked out the running man instantly and fired just as the man started to shout. The slug slammed his skull forward, and an eerie geyser of blood and brain tissue spattered the far wall of the tunnel as the body fell away from under the gory cloud.

Bolan started forward, cautiously damping the light against his hip. He heard nothing but his own footsteps. Letting a little light seep out, he stopped beside Randy to snatch his AK and a spare clip. Bolan ignored the remaining two bodies, stepping over the dead man with the flashlight. The light had gone on when he fell, and it lay in the water, its broken lens flecked with blood, turning the water a pale ruby color until the tube filled and the light died out.

"Strike two, Mr. Harding," Bolan said grimly as he headed toward the pale well of light up ahead.

28

The huge block of bright light floated above him like a square sun. Bolan heard several voices, all echoing down through the opening from some cavernous building nearly twenty feet overhead. The tunnel itself took the jumble of sound and garbled it still further. He looked at his watch, and read the dimly lit numerals—11:00. He had an hour.

Starting up the steel ladder, he held the Kalashnikov in his right hand, holding on to the rungs above him with one hand. Halfway up, shadow spilled down into the tunnel for a moment, and he froze as someone in fatigues stood almost on the lip of the entrance, his back to the hole.

The man bellowed at someone, then moved away, and Bolan let his breath out with a soft sigh. It was like climbing up from the bowels of the earth to an unknown place he'd never been. Every step brought him closer to the light. Every step brought him closer to Charles Harding.

Or to sudden death.

Near the top, he crouched to bring his feet up another rung. The AK cracked against the ladder, but the deafening din above swallowed the tolling of the metal strut. Leaning back, he could see the top of a corrugated sheet metal wall. The ceiling looked to be nearly fifty feet overhead. Craning his neck, he looked in the opposite direction, but that wall was too far away for him to see.

Bolan poked his head up over the floor. The warehouse was a jungle of steel shelving. A conveyor snaked through it like a stainless steel river, winding in and out among the shelves. Crates, easily recognizable as rifles and ammunition, sat in twos and threes on the silent, motionless conveyor, and pairs of men raced back and forth, lugging the crates to the open tailgates of a half-dozen trucks smeared in rippling camouflage patterns of greens, browns and black.

Waiting for the opportune moment, Bolan tested the spring in his legs and, when no one was looking, vaulted up onto the concrete floor. He ducked behind a stack of empty wooden crates, then wormed his way back away from the conveyor. It was almost impossible to gauge the number of men in the building. He needed a better vantage point.

High on the wall and about ten feet below the roof, a catwalk circled the building, and two others stretched from wall to wall, dividing the building into thirds. Another, made of the same metal slats, ran across the building at a right angle. At the center of each of the walls, a ladder climbed up to the catwalk. It was a hell of a choice, but there was no other.

Ducking under a branch of the serpentine conveyor, he moved through tall stacks of cartons and crates. He bent to crawl through a section of shelving bolted to the concrete floor, and crouched behind some crates stacked in an aisle. As near as he could tell, there must have been twenty men working the floor, and the vigilant top kick bellowing unintelligibly made twenty-one. So far, there was no sign of Harding or Cordero.

And unless they were there, it was pointless to take on a small army. The men scurrying around the floor were wheels going nowhere without the engine of Charles Harding to drive them. Bolan reached the far wall, which was draped in shadows from the towering stockpile and unlit by the fluorescent fixtures dangling directly overhead. Bolan moved along the wall, darting from stack to pile to stack.

At the corner he peered out from behind a pile of ruptured and discarded crates to the next corner, nearly three hundred feet away. A small cubicle, looking absurd and tiny in the cavernous interior of the warehouse, occupied the corner. Frosted glass concealed the interior of the cubicle, but it was as good a destination as any.

He started along the wall and nearly tripped over a man turning the corner, bent at the waist under the weight of a crate of ammunition. The startled man dropped the crate with a dull thud and cursed him. He glanced at Bolan angrily, then realized Bolan didn't belong there and went for the .45 automatic on his hip. Bolan dove at him, driving his injured shoulder into the man's gut and knocking him to the floor.

The smaller man struggled to throw him off, but Bolan slammed a fist into his windpipe, and he gagged. The gun clattered away, skidding across the cement. Bolan slugged him a second time, and the man's head snapped back into the concrete and he lay still.

Bolan got to his feet as someone shouted, "Enrique, where the hell is that ammo?" Bolan started to run as the shouting voice came closer, echoing among the boxes. He looked back just as the shouting man broke into the clear. Bolan dove behind a mound of canvas, but too late. He'd been spotted, and the pursuer came charging down the aisle, a pistol in his hand.

The man fired once, then two more quick shots. The slugs nipped at the canvas just over Bolan's head, then slammed into the corrugated wall, which boomed hollowly with the impacts. Bolan fired back, and his shot caught his target in the throat. The man clutched at his neck, and his legs stopped pumping, but the momentum carried him forward into the canvas, where he landed with a thud.

Bolan jumped to his feet and started to climb up the nearest stack of shelves, pulling himself from shelf to shelf and crawling into the center of the fourth tier, where he had just enough room to lie flat.

Several men came running from different parts of the warehouse, and Bolan held his breath. He snicked the safety off the Kalashnikov and waited. The men milled around in the aisle fifteen feet below, but no one seemed able to decide what to do.

One voice, coming from far behind him, cut through the babble. There was no mistaking its authority. "What the fuck is going on here?"

No one answered, and the voice barked again, even louder this time. "What's going on? Somebody start talking."

"We don't know, Colonel," someone stuttered, his voice faint and uncertain.

It was Charles Harding. Bolan felt a rising of energy, and a new alertness took hold of him. The quarry was in sight.

"Where's McAllister?" Harding snapped.

"There, sir."

Bolan heard shuffling feet as the men parted to give Harding an unobstructed view.

"What the hell happened?" Harding demanded. "Who did this?"

"Don't know, sir."

"Anybody see anything?"

Perfect silence. Bolan heard Harding's exasperated breathing for a few moments. Then he barked, "Johnson, pick eight men. Spread your asses out and look for the son of a bitch. Now! The rest of you get back to work. I want those trucks out of here in five minutes. Got it?"

"Yes, sir."

"I'll be in the command post if you need me. And you'd better *not*."

Bolan listened while Johnson made his selection, then the knot of men broke up and the feet shuffled off in every direction.

"All right, you two, down that end, one on either side. You two, same thing up this end. The rest of you, two teams of two, start there and sweep to the other end of this aisle. Anything moves, you kill it—I don't care if it's a cat. Find the bastard."

Bolan continued to hug the metal shelf, trying hard not to sneeze from the thick dust lying on the dull gray metal. One after another, the tailgates slammed shut. Bolan could hear the teams below him, whispering nervously as they peeked around corners and shoved piles of boxes aside, kicking likely hiding places and poking at empty boxes with their gun barrels.

A sound like thunder suddenly filled the huge building as the trucks fired up. Then, like an undercurrent of deeper, more distant thunder, one of the great doors moved up and out of the way. As the trucks started to roll, the floor of the building trembled, and the shelves picked up the vibrations. Loose bolts rattled like sizzles in a cymbal, and the entire building seemed to throb as if it were a single beast beginning to awaken.

With a grinding of gears, the first truck lumbered toward the door. It creaked under its load, and Bolan could only wonder where it was headed. The others followed, one by one, and he swiveled his body to try to see the door. A small triangle of visibility gave him just a glimpse of the last three freshly painted trucks. Then the door rattled shut again, the whine of its servo petulant, even testy, until it banged closed. The door trembled momentarily, and the sudden silence seemed more ominous than the thunder of the trucks.

"Find anything?" Johnson shouted, his voice—partly muffled by distance and the huge columns of material—strangely small under the high ceiling.

"Nothing."

"Keep looking!"

Bolan inched toward the edge of the shelf and raised his head just enough to look down into the far end of the aisle. The single man guarding that end lounged carelessly against a column. A few yards closer, one of the two-man search teams poked casually at some rubbish. Their enthusiasm seemed all but gone, replaced by the indifference of men going through the motions to please someone in authority.

Bolan's watch read 11:35. It was time to act. Muffling the click as best he could, Bolan replaced the partial clip in his Beretta 93-R with a full one. The sound suppressor gave him a slight edge, but the metal on which he lay afforded very little protection. If they saw him, it was all over.

Using a two-handed grip, he took aim on the lounging guard. The search team was almost at the end of the aisle. If they turned to work their way back, they might see him. It was now or never.

Squeezing the hair trigger, he felt the satisfying jolt of the Italian beauty, its deadly spit no louder than an apple falling on soft grass. The guard changed position, but seemed unharmed. Bolan thought for a moment the shot had missed. When the stain began to spread across the front of the guard's shirt, he knew he hadn't. The body stayed upright, propped against the rough metal.

Firing two more quick shots, Bolan took out the search team, catching the man on the left almost dead center, just below the collar line. A broken spine allowed his head to loll, and the man dropped straight down, dead instantly. The second man was no luckier. Struck in the base of the skull, he spattered his dead companion with flecks of bright blood and toppled to the floor, his weapon clattering against an empty metal drum.

"Hey!" The shout sparked like electricity through the aisles, and someone ran toward the fallen men, probably the guard from the opposite end of the aisle. Bolan couldn't see anyone, but took the opportunity to move to the other side of his perch. Pounding feet raced toward the end of the aisle, and as Bolan peeked out over the edge, he saw three men rushing toward the far end of the warehouse.

Checking both ways as the running men disappeared around a corner, Bolan climbed another shelf higher, then another. One more, and he'd be on top. The men far below seemed confused. He could hear their excited voices, and they appeared to be arguing among themselves what to do. Bolan took the plunge, grabbing the highest shelf and ignoring the stab of pain in his wounded shoulder as he hauled himself up.

"You better get the colonel," someone said, raising his voice to be heard over the hoarsely whispered argument.

"We don't tell him nothing, till we get the son of a bitch did this," Johnson snapped. "He'll have our asses, otherwise."

Bolan listened with half an ear as he considered his position. The aisles were wide. Wide enough for a forklift to maneuver among them. It was a good twelve feet. From a standing start, it was one hell of a broad jump.

But if he could get over two aisles, he could reach the catwalk.

"What the hell," he said.

And jumped.

The impact of his booted feet on the next shelf bounced around the girders above him like a sonic pinball. The metal and its echo made direction impossible to fix, and Bolan took the next leap and dropped to his stomach to wait before the noise had a chance to die down.

The men in the corner raced toward him, two aisles over. Picking the one spot that gave him a direct line among the shelves, he gripped the Beretta and waited for a target.

It wasn't long.

he first man flashed by. The second wasn't as fast . . . or as
lucky. The 9 mm slug bored down through his left shoulder, breaking the collarbone and ripping through a lung. He
fell like he'd been poleaxed.

Bolan crawled along the shelving toward its far end, getting to his feet and climbing onto a pair of wooden crates.
He left the AK-47 behind and launched himself straight up,
caught the edge of the catwalk and swung a leg up under the
safety rail. The M-16 dangled off his shoulder, its sling
sliding down along his upper arm.

Bolan swung his other leg up and lay flat on the catwalk.
The rifle still hung over the side, and someone spotted it. A
sudden burst of automatic rifle fire whistled past and
punched holes in the roof overhead. Rainwater started to
pour through the holes, its tepid warmth spattering the back
of his neck.

He tugged the rifle up onto the catwalk and sprang into a
crouch. As he ran, the catwalk swayed beneath him, and two
more weapons joined the attack. The slats of the catwalk
twinged as the hail of fire chewed at it. In the high shadows,
they couldn't see him, and he reached the far wall and
paused to catch his breath.

Moving quietly toward the dockside corner, he searched
the tangle below for a glimpse of the searchers. Dropping to
one knee, he zeroed in on the most likely spot, trying to

gauge the angle of fire. The shooting stopped, and he hear
running feet but nothing else.

Then, like silhouettes on a practice range, two men swun
into the open, their rifles ready and faces turned expe
tantly upward. Bolan cut loose with a tight burst, an
chopped one face to pieces, but the second man dodged be
hind cover. Bolan fired another burst, but the solid ham
mering of the slugs on the crating told him they weren
getting through. The man hadn't seen him, but it wouldn
be long. Surprise was no longer on his side.

Bolan started inching along the front wall, ducking un
der a pair of ventilation ducts. He could hear the slight hur
of the fans turned by the wind as it whistled past.

The search party was down to three, but he took no com
fort in the fact. He knew enough about probability to know
that the odds against him were still nine to one. Someon
fired a short nervous burst that ripped into the corner be
hind him, and Bolan smiled. They still didn't have a fix o
him.

A heavy door banged, and someone ran toward the cen
ter of the warehouse. Though it was out of his sight, Bola
knew from the sound that it was just one man.

When the voice boomed up into the shadowed corners, h
didn't have to guess who it was.

"Belasko, I know who you are." Harding sounded un
ruffled, even faintly amused. "You don't think you can ge
out of here alive, do you?" Harding laughed, and for
moment Bolan was tempted to take the bait.

"You don't have a prayer, Belasko. But I'll make you
deal. You ought to be with me, not against me. You know
that. I'm going to give you one minute. You hear that? Sixty
seconds. You can sign on, Belasko, and there'll be no har
feelings. If not, your ass is mine, mister. Think about it."

Bolan looked at his watch. It read 11:51. He didn't know whether Harding was stalling for time or not. But there was only one way to make sure. The middle catwalk was just thirty feet away. He moved toward it, waiting between steps to prevent the shaky platform from banging against the metal wall beside him.

At the intersection he eased out onto the narrow walkway. His weight made it squeak slightly, and he held his breath for a moment.

"Thirty seconds, cowboy."

Another five steps, and he could see two men: Johnson and one of the two remaining members of the search team. Two more steps and he had a clean shot. He steadied the Beretta on the safety rail. Squeezing once, he jerked the muzzle and squeezed again.

When he looked, Johnson was nowhere to be seen. A fatigue-clad arm, its hand twitching spastically, was barely visible at the edge of a wooden crate. He couldn't tell whether it was Johnson or the other man, and he didn't know whether he'd gotten them both. But that was not the question.

Where was Harding?

That was the question.

"Ten seconds, Belasko. Nine . . . eight . . . seven . . ."

And he broke for the far wall, the catwalk swaying beneath him like the deck of a plunging boat in high seas.

"Kill him!" Harding shouted. Gunfire, as near as he could tell from only two weapons, ripped at the metal slats, punching holes in the aluminum and scattering sharp slivers in every direction.

He was willing to bet they expected him to take the ladder. Bolan reached the far wall and ran toward the ladder a few steps, then stopped. He cut back, remembering the thick bundle of canvas. He spotted it, nearly twenty-five feet on the ladder's far side. One of the huge doors rumbled oper then an engine sprang to life.

The jeep raced its engine, then jerked into gear. "Yo hear that, Belasko? It's over, sport. Time's up."

The jeep's tires squealed on the concrete, and a burst c gunfire echoed through the warehouse as Bolan leapt. Be fore he touched down, he heard the jeep slam into the wal its engine racing under a lead foot, the tires screamin against the cement, then the engine died.

Bolan hit and rolled. As he came up, Johnson and th other man turned their rifles on him, but Bolan was just little quicker. He emptied a clip, then jerked the wasted cli free and jammed in another.

Bolan sprinted past the twitching bodies and careere around a corner. He caught a glimpse of Harding just be fore the man vanished. Someone fired a shot, and Hardin returned the fire with two quick ones from an automati pistol. Bolan reached the aisle and ran into Carlos, nearl knocking him over, just as Harding rounded the far corne In surprise, Bolan turned, reaching out to steady the youn Filipino. Behind him he saw a bright flash of light, then went dark.

The clunk of the master switch echoed through the ware house.

"Carlos, what are you doing here?" Bolan whispered.

"The police are coming soon. Señora Colgan, she sai you needed help. She led me through the tunnel. When w came up, I saw the jeep starting to leave. It was Cordero."

"Was?"

"I killed him, Señor Belasko."

That left Harding himself. Swat him like the bug he was wipe your hands, and walk away, Bolan thought. That's a there was to it.

But first he had to find Harding. And that wouldn't be easy in the dark.

Bolan heard the footsteps, and clapped a hand over Carlos' mouth. "Shhh. Listen, you find Señora Colgan, and you stay with her. Sit on her if you have to, but don't leave her alone. And whatever she says, don't let her talk you into anything. Understand?"

Carlos nodded, and as Bolan relaxed the pressure, Carlos whispered, *"Si, señor."*

He heard Carlos move away, back down the aisle toward where he'd seen Marisa just before the lights went out. The concrete underfoot, covered with sand and hunks of wood, papers and the usual sort of litter, made too much noise under his soles. Bolan unlaced his boots and kicked them off, then moved toward the wall. He hadn't had time to check the warehouse, and Harding had a distinct advantage in knowing the layout. When his outstretched fingers brushed against the rough metal of the wall, Bolan hesitated.

Which way should he go?

Harding was an unconventional strategist. And if that weren't enough, he was also desperate. Behind him he heard a strange sound, almost like running water, and he wondered whether something might be happening in the tunnel beneath the warehouse. But there was no point in worrying about what might happen. He had a ruthless killer loose somewhere in the dark, and at the moment, that was the only thing that mattered.

Bolan groped along the wall and nearly shouted when he stepped on something sharp. The pain shot through his foot, and when he lifted it, he felt a piece of crating come off the floor, pinned to the foot by a nail.

He bent the leg, cradled the foot against his knee and, balancing on one foot, jerked the slat free. He set it down

gingerly, then tried to put some weight on the puncture
foot. A fierce stab of pain shot up the calf, and he balled hi
toes instinctively to take some of his weight off the wound
It would slow him down.

But it wouldn't stop him.

Only one thing could do that, and he wasn't ready for tha
yet.

He continued along the wall as footsteps scraped on th
sandy floor somewhere in the distance. Again, that gurgle
and again he pushed it out of his mind. Concentrate, h
whispered—first things first. Concentrate, damn it. He ig
nored the pain in his foot, the aching shoulder. In his mind
a white-hot light, like the headlight of an approachin
freight train, burned brightly. Outlined in that brillian
glare, he could see Charles Harding. There was nothing an
no one else.

Bolan stepped on the corner of a piece of lumber, and th
point stabbed at the puncture wound. He convulsed in
stinctively, bending to grab the foot, and it saved his life. /
sharp crack resounded throughout the warehouse, right be
hind the awful crunch of a slug punching through the rust
metal wall right where his head had been. Bolan dove to th
floor, forgetting about the pain, and wondered how in th
hell Harding could see him.

He scrambled forward several feet, slithering like a liz
ard, then jumped to his feet. Moving faster, he heard foot
steps scrape across the floor, and that strange gurgling
again. His fingers bumped against a metal box mounted on
the wall. It echoed hollowly like a drum, and he knew im
mediately what it was.

Groping along the box, he found the handle and
wrenched it up with a jerk of his wrist. The fluorescent
flickered overhead, strobing a moment, flashing a strange
blue-gray light before snapping fully on.

Bolan blinked away the glare and turned. He saw Harding and ducked just as another shot sailed past him. And Bolan's gut clenched like a fist. He knew now how Harding had seen him. The night-vision glasses vised the man's head, sprouts of gray hair shooting up like weeds under the pressure of the elastic band.

In Harding's right hand, he saw a big Colt .45. Its blued steel gleamed under the light.

But that wasn't the problem.

Harding's left hand was clenched tightly over Marisa Colgan's mouth. She struggled, but Harding was too strong for her, dragging her along in his powerful grip, with just her toes scraping the floor. Bolan waved his Beretta back and forth, the mesmerizing sway of a flute before a cobra.

But he didn't have a clear shot.

"Let her go, Harding."

Harding laughed. "Not in this life, Belasko," he spat. "Not in this life."

Marisa continued to struggle, but it was useless. Harding was just too strong. The big Colt cracked again, this time punching into a crate just in front of Bolan's shoulder. The slug glanced off something inside the crate and rocacheted out through the side of the thin wooden container.

A shot cracked behind him. As Harding turned, momentarily relaxing his grip, Marisa chomped down hard on the slack fingers. Harding howled as Marisa spun away, and Bolan fired once.

The bullet slammed into Harding's skull, leaving a small black hole in his temple, then blasting a softball-sized exit on its way out the other side. Marisa lay there moaning as Bolan charged forward. He checked to see that she wasn't hurt, and she reached for him. "I'm all right," she said. "Really, I'm all right." Bolan helped her up and supported her weight, feeling the frightened tremble.

He glanced at the bloody shambles that had been Harding's head, then turned away. Down the aisle, Carlos, a pool of blood from his slashed throat already coagulating on the concrete, stared back at him with glazed, sightless eyes. His fingers still curved around the pistol, but they no longer felt it.

"Carlos," Marisa whispered. "Where's Carlos?"

Bolan shook his head. "Gone," he said.

He started walking, holding Marisa close. She buried her head in his shoulder and sobbed quietly. He passed through the huge door out into the Manila night. Out in the harbor, a giant freighter drifted behind a laboring tug. A single mournful blast of its horn shattered the night, then left it stiller than before. For once, Bolan didn't mind the thick air, the clinging tropical humidity.

"That's one score settled," he said to the night.

DON PENDLETON's
MACK BOLAN®

More SuperBolan bestseller action! Longer than the monthly series, SuperBolans feature Mack in more intricate, action-packed plots— more of a good thing

		Quantity
STONY MAN DOCTRINE follows the action of paramility strike squads, Phoenix Force and Able Team.	$3.95	☐
RESURRECTION DAY renews a long-standing war against the Mafia.	$3.95	☐
DIRTY WAR follows the group on a secret mission into Cambodia.	$3.95	☐
DEAD EASY tracks down an elusive but deadly Mafia-KGB connection.	$3.95	☐

Total Amount	$	
Plus 75¢ Postage		.75
Payment enclosed		

Please send a check or money order payable to Gold Eagle Books.

In the U.S.A.	In Canada	SMB-2A
Gold Eagle Books 901 Fuhrmann Blvd. Box 1325 Buffalo, NY 14269-1325	Gold Eagle Books P.O. Box 609 Fort Erie, Ontario L2A 5X3	 GOLD EAGLE®

Please Print

Name: _____

Address: _____

City: _____

State/Prov: _____

Zip/Postal Code: _____

TAKE 'EM NOW

FOLDING SUNGLASSES
FROM GOLD EAGLE

Mean up your act with these tough, street-smart shades. Practical, too, because they fold 3 times into a handy, zip-up polyurethane pouch that fits neatly into your pocket. Rugged metal frame. Scratch-resistant acrylic lenses. Best of all, they can be yours for only $6.99.
MAIL YOUR ORDER TODAY.

Send your name, address, and zip code, along with a check or money order for just $6.99 + .75¢ for delivery (for a total of $7.74) payable to Gold Eagle Reader Service.
(New York residents please add applicable sales tax.)

Remove from pouch...

unfold once...

Gold Eagle Reader Service
3010 Walden Avenue
P.O. Box 1396
Buffalo, N.Y. 14240-1396

unfold twice...

and they're ready to wear.

GES-1AR

Offer not available in Canada.

Phoenix Force—bonded in secrecy to avenge the acts of terrorists everywhere

SEARCH AND DESTROY $3.95   ☐

American "killer" mercenaries are involved in a KGB plot to overthrow the government of a South Pacific island. The American President, anxious to preserve his country's image and not disturb the precarious position of the island nation's government, sends in the experts—Phoenix Force—to prevent a coup.

FIRE STORM $3.95   ☐

An international peace conference turns into open warfare when terrorists kidnap the American President and the premier of the USSR at a summit meeting. As a last desperate measure Phoenix Force is brought in—for if demands are not met, a plutonium core device is set to explode.

Total Amount	$	_____
Plus 75¢ Postage		.75
Payment enclosed	$	_____

Please Print

Name: _____

Address: _____

City: _____

State/Prov: _____

Zip/Postal Code: _____

GOLD EAGLE

SPF-A

DON PENDLETON's

MACK BOLAN®

The line between good and evil is a tightrope no man should walk. Unless that man is the Executioner.

TIGHTROPE $3.95   ☐
When top officials of international Intelligence agencies are murdered, Mack Bolan pits his skill against an alliance of renegade agents and uncovers a deadly scheme to murder the U.S. President.

MOVING TARGET $3.95   ☐
America's most powerful corporations are reaping huge profits by dealing in arms with anyone who can pay the price. Dogged by assassins, Mack Bolan becomes caught in a power struggle that might be his last.

FLESH & BLOOD $3.95   ☐
When Asian communities are victimized by predators among their own—thriving gangs of smugglers, extortionists and pimps—they turn to Mack Bolan for help.

Total Amount	$ _____
Plus 75¢ Postage	_____.75
Payment enclosed	$ _____

Please send a check or money order payable to Gold Eagle Books.

In the U.S.	In Canada
Gold Eagle Books	Gold Eagle Books
901 Fuhrmann Blvd.	P.O. Box 609
Box 1325	Fort Erie, Ontario
Buffalo, NY 14269-1325	L2A 5X3

GOLD EAGLE

Please Print
Name: _____
Address: _____
City: _____
State/Prov: _____
Zip/Postal Code: _____

SMB-3R

Do you know a real hero?